Praise for The Z

Great Book, Hard to Put Down

"I loved this book, and I don't normally read zombie books. The first few chapters were confusing to me but once both storylines converged, it got so interesting I could not put it down."

Another Action-Packed Explosion from Lance!

"Another blast of a read!! Pulls you in from page one. You just start to relax getting to know the characters and bam!!! The action explodes and doesn't stop until the last page."

Amazing Read

"Well, the author has done it again, an amazing story which grips you from the start. it starts with a softer side then, it takes a turn and then you can't put the book down. it was that good I read the book twice, I can't recommend this book enough. The book is outstanding and full of excitement. great work lance looking forward to the next one."

Ready for the next book already, keep them Coming!

A real page-turner and another thrilling read!

"This was such a good book. I'm hoping for another book as this definitely needs to be a series. Well worth a read and definitely see the other books by this author."

Lance Winkless was born in Sutton Coldfield, England, brought up in Plymouth, Devon and now lives in Staffordshire with his partner and daughter.

For more information on Lance Winkless and future writing see his website.

www.LanceWinkless.com

By Lance Winkless

THE CAPITAL FALLING TRILOGY

CAPITAL FALLING
CAPITAL FALLING 2 – DENIAL
CAPITAL FALLING 3 – RESURGENCE

THE Z SEASON – TRILOGY

KILL TONE
VOODOO SUN
CRUEL FIX

Visit Amazon Author Pages

Amazon US - Amazon.com/author/lancewinkless
Amazon UK - Amazon.co.uk/-/e/B07QJV2LR3

Why Not Follow

Facebook www.facebook.com/LanceWinklessAuthor
Twitter @LanceWinkless
Instagram @LanceWinkless
Pinterest www.pinterest.com/lancewinkless
BookBub www.bookbub.com/authors/lance-winkless

ALL REVIEWS POSTED ARE VERY MUCH APPRECIATED, THEY ARE SO IMPORTANT, THANKS

CRUEL FIX

Enjoy Liz

Lance Winkless

Published by Lance Winkless

www.LanceWinkless.com

Onset

The faint ping of a pin hitting the tiled floor might be heard—if one were dropped—in the virtual silence of the laboratory-come-classroom over which Jonathan Bradley is presiding. His young pupils know better than to break his silence; even the merest snigger or hint of chatter would result in his wrath bearing down on the perpetrator. The poor, guilty child would then be trapped into spending additional time, their free time, in *Sir's* unwanted company.

This class of little shits is still young and innocent enough to be held under Mr Bradley's spell. The kids aren't yet equipped to attempt to push back against his tyrannical rule, and there aren't many older pupils who would dare to test him either.

The class's torrid hour of chemistry with Mr Bradley is all but over, and the bell will ring in a few minutes' time. No pupil risks raising their head from the textbook in front of them, however; not until Bradley gives the word.

Looking at the clock hanging on the whitewashed wall, Bradley fixes on the second hand as it clicks towards the top. With two minutes and five seconds to go until the bell sounds, Bradley's head turns to his class whose heads are all still lowered.

"Pack up your belongings," he tells the class in a monotone voice.

The incessant bustle of children packing their books and pencil cases into their bags rises immediately.

"Quietly," Bradley announces, annoyed at the sudden noise even though none of the children has uttered a word, not even to their best friend, their fear keeping their lips shut tight.

Bradley mirrors the children, sliding his papers and books into his carry case, ready to follow the children out of the laboratory. Pupils start to file past Bradley's desk, eager to get out from under his gaze, and a few hushed words are exchanged as the children finally cross the threshold and exit the foreboding room. Not one of the pupils approaches Bradley or goes to ask a question; they don't even cast a glance his way, which is just the way he likes it.

The school bell has sounded, and his work is done.

It's always the same little bleeders who bring up the rear, Bradley thinks as the last child leaves, and he can finally shut and lock the door. At last, his day of enlightening ungrateful children is over. There is one last thing to take care of before he can get in his car and drive away for the weekend, and that thing is something he will do secretly, once the other members of staff have shot off ready to start their insignificant weekends.

Striding down the hall, any children in his path quickly get out of his way, his mere presence enough to make them swerve, their eyes darting to the floor.

His fellow teachers don't cause him to break his stride either; they move just the same, even if they do offer him a nod in greeting, with stern faces.

Bradley takes the stairs quickly up to the next floor, his worn, brown, rubber-soled shoes squeaking against the aluminium stripped steps as he goes. The upper level is now deserted; teachers and pupils alike have left as quickly as possible to start their weekend of freedom.

A hefty bunch of keys jangles out of Bradley's front trouser pocket and he expertly fingers through them with one hand. The required key is between his thumb and index finger by the time he reaches the door to the science block's storage room, and he slides it straight into the lock. Bradley's head turns nervously up and down the corridor, checking that the coast is clear as he turns the key and pushes the door open.

Inside, he swiftly pulls the key out and pushes against the door, to close it quickly and quietly. Nobody saw him enter, Bradley is sure of that. Not that it matters; he is the head of department and quite entitled to be in the storeroom.

Questions might be asked, however, about why he was entering at this time on a Friday. Bradley knows that, it's in his mind. He could easily find an excuse if he were to be asked, or he could just tell the busybody to mind their own business.

Nevertheless, Bradley ignores the light switch on the wall and goes over to the door to the storage room proper; there's no need to draw attention by lighting up the preparation area.

Cool air wafts out of the storage room as the seal between the two rooms is broken.

Bradley steps inside, and this time, he has to flick the switch to turn on the lights since there are no windows inside this space.

Strip lights flicker for a moment before they light up, to illuminate the racks of chemicals and equipment held securely there, all ready to be distributed to the science lessons.

Bradley is well aware that everything on the racks in front of him is accounted for and documented, but he also knows that the odd gram or millilitre syphoned away is not noticed or will be overlooked by the technicians responsible. He has been helping himself to small amounts of the ingredients he needs for his own experiments for quite some time, and is careful not to get greedy. He is very selective too; almost everything he needs can be ordered online, bought from specialist outlets, or even from his local supermarket.

Only the specialist chemicals that cannot be purchased 'over the counter', or those that would draw attention if ordered, does he acquire from the racks in front of him. Many people would be surprised at what chemicals and agents are kept in a school's science department.

Lifting his carry case, Bradley pulls the zip open and delves inside, his fingers wrapping around two small plastic bottles. His eyes have located his first target before his hand emerges from inside the bag: a white plastic container that would be nondescript if it weren't for the skull and crossbones printed on its label.

Placing the bottles onto the shelf next to the container of arsenic, Bradley goes back into his bag to find the small spatula nestled at the bottom.

Picking up one of his small plastic bottles, Bradley unscrews its lid ready to receive its cargo. Then, spatula at the ready, he carefully unscrews the lid from the container holding his prize. The yellow powder that Bradley dips his small spatula into looks innocent enough, and could be mistaken for mustard powder. Scooping up a little of the poisonous arsenic powder with his spatula, he carefully moves the scoop over to the waiting bottle and pours the powder in. Repeating the process twice more, he then replaces the bottle top. He daren't help himself to more than three scoops, an amount he is satisfied won't raise any alarms.

Ensuring the bottle top is secured, Bradley drops the bottle into his open carry case and goes over to the washbasin to swill off his spatula.

Not needing the spatula for his next acquisition, Bradley now drops it into the opening of his case and quickly finds the bottle of dioxane he is looking for. Taking it from its perch on the rack, he goes back to the basin, where he proceeds to pour the re-agenting liquid carefully into his small bottle, filling it halfway.

With the second bottle's lid tightened, Bradley puts it in his carry case and pulls its zip shut. He replaces the bottle of dioxane and then moves to the door to exit. He takes one last look behind him to double-check nothing is out of place, and then flicks off the light switch.

The corridor is deserted when he shuts the door to the storage room, which locks itself quietly behind him. A feeling of satisfaction and anticipation grows in his gut as he strides down the corridor to make his way out of the building and start his weekend, just as everyone else in the building already seems to have done.

The sun has made a reappearance, which Bradley relishes as he steps out of the science block and into the surprisingly warm December afternoon. The warmth won't last, however, and the sun that is already starting to dip in the sky tells him that. Nevertheless, Bradley allows himself to enjoy the sun on his face as he walks across the courtyard in front of the science block, and towards the staff car park. He has 'acquired' his chemicals, and he now has a productive, if not challenging weekend to look forward to.

"Have a good weekend," some of the staff members say to him as he walks.

Bradley at least nods in reply to them. *I must be in a good mood*, he thinks. Most of the cars have already departed the staff carpark when he arrives, and it isn't long before he is unlocking his pushbike and pedalling towards the exit.

Bradley only brings his car into school if the weather forecast says it is going to be wet.

He much prefers cycling; he only lives ten minutes away, and it can take just as long to drive in when the roads are jammed with parents' cars on the school run.

More importantly, it is the only real form of exercise he gets; there is no gym membership for him, and even the thought of one fills him with dread.

Some might call Bradley's bike old-fashioned; he likes to think of it as a classic. Either way, it certainly wasn't built for speed and that suits him fine, he enjoys gliding along at a steady pace, no matter how many disgruntled drivers he holds up on his travels.

He savours taking in the scenery and views as he rides along the outskirts of the small, middle-England city of Lemsfield, which is no bigger than most towns. The only reason Lemsfield is classed as a city is because of the large, Gothic cathedral that the city has grown around over the centuries, its three towering spires visible from miles around.

The outskirts of the city are soon behind him as Bradley coasts into the small city centre, where he lives. Every time he arrives at the centre, it reminds him of when he and his wife, Wendy, first moved to Lemsfield over ten years ago.

They visited the city many times before moving here, and always loved it, with its picturesque, historic, centre that was always bustling with locals and visitors alike.

Here, throughout the summer and even into the winter, events are held in and around the city to attract visitors and tourists. The food and beer festivals were their favourite, but there are so many more events to draw people in, from music festivals to traditional parades through the city. There is always something going on in the city and even when there's no specific event, people still flock from neighbouring towns and villages to soak up the atmosphere provided by the plethora of pubs and restaurants, and to experience the lively nightlife.

When Bradley was offered the chance of a teaching position at the local high school—almost ten years ago—he and his wife jumped at the chance and moved, lock, stock, and barrel. Those were marvellous times, a virtually new life for him and Wendy.

They jumped into it with both feet.

A car behind revs its engine, the driver becoming impatient with Bradley's ambling progress, but he takes no notice. In fact, his legs stop pedalling as he approaches the upmarket street they moved into all those years ago.

The bike's speed slows more, but Bradley doesn't turn into the street. With a heavy heart, he drifts past the turning, and with a glance as he passes, and finally starts pedalling again.

It has been over a year since he moved out of his beloved house, since he discovered Wendy's affair, and his new life of torment began.

Bradley's legs suddenly start to pump his pedals vigorously, and to the relief of the new driver stuck behind him, his speed picks up as it always does after he passes that street.

At his increased speed, it's not long before he reaches the rented house he was forced to move into after his marriage hit the rocks. Nowadays, Bradley is never happy to get home, not even after the most stressful of days with the little brats at school.

It's not that the house is unpleasant; it's presentable and situated on the very cusp of the city centre and all it has to offer, but it's just not home, only a place to exist.

Dismounting his bike, Bradley squeezes it past his car—parked on the small, narrow drive—and chains it up in its spot at the front of the house, before he covers it with its waterproof cover. The front door bangs shut as Bradley drops his carry case on the carpet, that he didn't choose, next to the bottom of the stairs.

Forty-seven years old and what have I got to show for it? Living in a rented house with nobody to welcome me home, he thinks as he climbs the stairs to take a shower.

Showered and changed, Bradley comes down with an eagerness to carry on with his 'project', the anger at the injustice of his situation driving him to places he couldn't have imagined in his previous life. He quickly has the two bottles containing his most recent acquisitions in his hand and takes them through to the kitchen. Placing the bottles on the work surface, his first task is to put the kettle on; he works much better with a cup of tea to hand.

While the kettle is boiling, he unlocks the padlock that he has fitted to one of the kitchen cabinets, the cabinet that stores the other supplies he needs for his project.

An array of bottles and scientific equipment is sitting inside the cabinet, some of the bottles having also been 'acquired' from the school's science block, but most have been acquired quite legitimately. Before he takes anything out, he waits for the kettle to boil, leaning his backside against the work surface. For a moment, he lets his mind wander in contemplation.

The kettle clicks off, pulling him out of his dark thoughts and almost making him jump. He fills his mug with boiling water and lets it sit for a minute, before pouring the hot water down the sink. Only when he is satisfied that his mug is hot enough does he proceed to make his tea, and then leaves the teabag stewing for a good two minutes before fishing it out.

Finally, with his tea-making ritual complete and the mug sitting steaming next to him, Bradley begins to start taking items out of the cabinet.

Bradley uses the gas burners on the stove as his Bunsen burner.

He has adapted a tripod stand from school to stand over the flames, and soon has his unique concoction simmering away in the beaker on top of the stand.

Periodically, and at specific times, he adds more ingredients into the beaker, including the arsenic and dioxane he stole from the science block storage room earlier. Bradley is very particular in ensuring he exactly follows his notes, written down in front of him. It has taken quite some time and a good deal of trial and error to develop his serum, and he finally thinks it is starting to work. Occasionally, the process or compounds added will be adjusted, or fine-tuned as it is perfected, but overall, its results are becoming very encouraging.

His mug of tea long since emptied, Bradley turns off the gas to allow the serum to cool slowly, and while it does, he carefully clears up the work surface in readiness to prepare dinner.

The tomato pasta dish doesn't take long for him to knock up, not that he is hungry, at least not yet. Steam rises from the mound on the plate, and Bradley runs the tap for a cold glass of water while he adds the finishing touches to the pasta.

The beaker is still warm to the touch, but he doesn't burn his fingers when he lifts it from the tripod. Raising the beaker to his nose, he gives it a sniff, as if it were a vintage glass of wine; he doesn't take a sip though, as the bouquet is pungent.

Bradley lowers it to the pasta and carefully pours the contents over the top, circling the beaker around, ensuring the light-yellow liquid is spread evenly over the pasta. He continues until the last drop of serum drips from the rim of the beaker.

He puts the empty beaker straight into the sink under the flow of cold water and leaves it there, the water overflowing out of the beaker top.

Opening the top cabinet in front of him, Bradley takes out a grinder of chilli and twists it until the pasta has a generous sprinkling of flakes covering it. Then, using two forks, he mixes the plate of withering worms until he is satisfied the chilli will mask any untoward flavours. With the meal complete, he fills a glass with the cold water and places it on the tray above the fork and spoon that sit next to the steaming plate.

Chapter 1

Carefully picking up the tray, Bradley carries it out into the hall, turning left. Nestled under the stairs is a door that could easily be missed—and not only because it has several coats hanging on the front of it. Balancing one side of the tray on his right arm, he reaches with his hand to open the door to the basement and flicks on the light switch.

When Bradley had first viewed the house, the agent who showed him around had raved about the basement, about its size and how useful it would be.

He wasn't convinced that it would be much use, not to him anyway, and when he had first moved in, he'd almost forgotten about it.

It was only after a few weeks that it had piqued his interest; he had always wanted a 'man cave'. Wendy, however, had never understood why he would even consider it.

She'd almost taken offence when he'd mentioned it.

"Why do you want a room for yourself? Don't you want to be with me?" she questioned, and so that was the end of that. But nothing was stopping him from having a man cave now, and the basement was the perfect place to create one—and so he did.

Descending the narrow stairs and trying not to crack your head on the low ceiling is tricky with a tray of food and a drink, but Bradley is well versed in it now, and nothing is spilled when he reaches the bottom. A faint feeling of satisfaction rises in him as he enters his domain. The house is rented and above the basement, it is decorated to somebody else's taste.

The furniture up there is his, but even that is mostly second-hand, already soiled by somebody else. It's amazing how poor you can find yourself when your marriage breaks up, and second hand was all he could afford, apart from his bed.

He certainly wasn't going to sleep on somebody else's bug-ridden mattress.

He had tried to be magnanimous with Wendy, had tried to appease her and get on her good side by letting her keep almost everything in the house. Where had that got him?

Did she remember how much they loved each other?

Did she see the error of her ways and try to reconcile? No! It got him absolutely fucking nowhere. Some other cunt settled into his lovely house, got to enjoy his hard-earned furniture, got to sleep and fuck his wife in the bed he had assembled, and that cunt's name was *Brian.*

***

Taking a breath, Bradley walks over to the desk he has built adjacent to the near wall and puts the tray down in front of the large computer screen mounted there.

He stands and looks around his basement, as he always does; he always needs a minute to calm down when he gets down here. It doesn't take long before his heart rate drops, the calming influence of the basement doing the trick. Everything down here is new, and it is his, from the flat-screen TV hung on the wall, to the small couch opposite it.

He even repainted the whole room and laid new carpet before he started to fit it out.

The meal is getting cold, I'd better get to it, Bradley thinks, and goes over to the opposite side of the basement.

The construction he has carried out at the other end of the basement is his crowning achievement; it took six weeks in total to finish, but the results couldn't have been better.

Bradley reaches his hand over to the wall, presses in, and slides across a secret compartment hidden at the very edge, in the corner, where it and the adjoining wall meet.

Buried in the wall is a padlock into which he inserts a key and turns it, allowing the padlock to snap open. Unhooking the padlock, Bradley pulls at the wall.

A hiss of air sounds as the seal is broken and the wall starts to move.

As if by magic, the whole wall at the end of the basement glides inwards into the middle, cantilevering and folding in two. New light streams into the basement as Bradley pushes the hidden door across until it folds flat against the adjacent wall. What once looked like a solid wall now reveals a completely hidden room at the end of the basement.

A metal grille straddles the entire width of the basement, securing the hidden room. In the centre of the grille is another door, also meshed steel, and behind is an area measuring precisely two-meters deep by approximately three-and-a-half-meters wide, the width of the basement.

Bradley takes a step back to once more marvel at his workmanship, and then to check that everything is as it should be inside his secret compartment.

"Wendy," Bradley says soothingly, not wanting to frighten his wife who is lying on the small bed behind the mesh. For a moment, Wendy doesn't acknowledge his call, and she stays completely still. Bradley moves down onto his haunches until his face is opposite and almost at the same level as hers. "Wendy," he says again, staring into his wife's beautiful face, her head resting on her two hands that are in prayer against the mattress.

"Are you hungry? I've made your favourite pasta dish," Bradley says.

Having no other option, Wendy has to control her fear and anger, and she has to stop pretending she is asleep and flickers her eyes open to look at her monstrous, estranged husband.

He stares at her through the squares of metal that separate them, his disgusting face smiling, with a look of joy at seeing her. "There you go sleepyhead," Bradley says as Wendy's eyes open and she forces a smile at him. "I've made you pasta, but I'll clean your room before I bring it in."

Getting up, Bradley moves over to the mesh door and unlocks it. He can see that her bucket has its lid on, meaning she has had a number two in it.

He doesn't mind clearing it up for her, and goes in to retrieve the bucket as Wendy moves into a sitting position on her bed under her duvet.

"That's heavy," Bradley jokes as he picks up the bucket, takes it out, and puts it down near the stairs. "Look at this, freshly made pasta, tomato and chilli," he announces as he picks up the tray from his desk. The dread at the thought of the food fills Wendy's aching body.

Even her deep, gnawing hunger isn't enough to stop her gagging on the poison she is well aware Jonathan is feeding her. He will sit at the end of her bed watching her intently while she eats, and he won't move until she has finished the entire meal—no matter how long she takes to eat it and how many of her gags she has to swallow and hide.

Wendy's weakening stomach turns as her captor approaches with her heinous meal.

She doesn't know how long she can carry on this pretence, as her body is failing and she can feel her life ebbing away.

She has no idea what her once charming husband is mixing in with her evening meal; it could be anything, knowing his scientific background. His goal is obvious though.

He tried to win her back but failed, so now he is attempting to drug her into submission, trying to turn her into a mindless zombie he can easily control. And he is winning. It isn't only her body that is failing; her mind is disintegrating with every minute she is locked in her dungeon, and with every mouthful of poison she is forced to consume.

"Here you go, my love," Jonathan says to her as he leans over to place the tray on her lap. "You must be hungry, what with me being at work all day. I'm sorry I can't be here for you in the week, but it's the weekend now, so I can spend lots more time with you." He smiles.

Lucky me. As much as I hate this dungeon you have made for me, I'd rather be in it alone than with you, Wendy thinks.

If only that were completely true, but she knows it is not. Even spending time with her vile captor is a release from the hours of monotony that have been her existence for these past weeks. If she can eat this food, she may even get to leave her cell and go upstairs, and be allowed to take the shower she has craved the whole day.

Just the smell of tomato and chilli drifting up to her nose is enough to make Wendy's stomach convulse. No matter how much chilli he has sprinkled into the meal, it doesn't completely hide the toxic smell of whatever the pasta is laced with.

Steeling herself, Wendy picks up the fork and then the spoon, her stomach muscles tightening to hold her belly in place. Wrapping the first strands of pasta around her fork, she glances up at the cook, sitting on the end of her bed. His face is one of encouragement, yet trepidation, as if he were a renowned chef watching a customer about to taste his latest addition to the menu, for the first time. Wendy clears her mind and lifts the fork to her mouth, her concentration absolute as the moist pasta touches her lips and enters her mouth.

Bradley watches Wendy intently as she eats, and he wonders if she realises that she is consuming his serum? Either way, he feels satisfaction with every mouthful she swallows, each one bringing her closer to becoming his again. He is convinced that the serum is working.

She is no longer aggressive towards him, and she smiles at him, her eyes sometimes watching him almost as they used to. He even managed to touch her foot yesterday as she was getting back into bed. She didn't recoil from his touch, not immediately anyway.

He can see that she is changing and becoming more placid, that the drugs are changing her. Once her treatment is complete, she won't be the woman she once was, strong-willed and feisty; he knows that, and he isn't stupid.

She will be calm and forgiving, devoted to him, she will be his and his alone.

When that happens, he will worship her, body and mind, and his anticipation to worship her body is profound but he will wait until the time is right, until she is ready to receive him.

"Did you enjoy that?" Bradley asks when Wendy places the fork and spoon down onto the empty plate.

"Yes, thank you," Wendy lies, as her ordeal is finally complete. "You know pasta is my favourite."

"Yes, of course, I do, my love, and I like making it for you," Bradley says, as he lifts the tray from her lap. "Shall we watch some television while your food goes down?"

"Yes, please," Wendy replies, her belly aching and somersaulting as it digests its torrid payload. She would dearly love to be able to ask to take her shower now, so that she could put her head down the toilet and vomit the poison from her body. Jonathan would not agree though, not again. The sound of the shower didn't cover the sound of her retching when she had done it previously—some weeks ago—and he had heard her being sick.

When she had emerged from the bathroom, he was annoyed and asked her if she had been sick. Too afraid to lie, she had told him she had, it had just happened, that she might have a bug or something, and not that she had stuck her fingers as far as possible down the back of her throat.

Since then, he has always made a point of asking her if she wants to watch television while her food goes down. When it is shower time, it will be too late; the food will be too far down to vomit up, at least not quietly.

For the next hour, Jonathan sits on his couch watching nondescript American comedies. Wendy moves from her bed to the chair opposite, to make a show of watching the television with him. She knows that he watches her move, his eyes fixed on her body, barely covered by the short nighties that are the only thing he gives her to wear.

He never puts anything of interest on the TV for them to watch, apart from the occasional nature programme, a conscious effort on his part to not let her watch the news or anything current. He hates these types of mindless comedies, and would never watch them with her even when they were together.

She doesn't care what's on the TV or if he is ogling her.

All she cares about is what is happening to her body. The feeling of sickness is something she has become quite used to; it is the norm.

Her lower stomach is starting to digest his poison though. She can feel it entering her bloodstream and it burns her veins. Her legs are on fire.

The muscles in her arms contract painfully as contaminated blood pumps into them and circulates higher through her body. Crunching sounds enter her head when her spine spasms tightly until it goes rigid, nearly toppling her from the chair below her. Toxins flow up through the sides of her neck, forcing the arteries and veins there to swell outwards, their dark blue colour appearing as bruises along the length of her slender neck.

A whimper escapes her lips when the dirty blood finally enters her brain, that bulges against her skull in protest, threatening to burst. The pain causing her vision to blur, and eventually, blackout. Wendy's head cries out in excruciating pain, a whining noise resonating from deep within her throat, the pain that is too much to bear suddenly cuts off.

"Wendy, Wendy, are you okay?" his vile voice vibrates into her eardrum, her consciousness returning. *Fuck off and leave me alone*, her mind screams, *leave me here to die, you horrible man*, but he won't.

"Wendy," he says again, his rank breath entering her nostrils as he pulls at her, trying to lift her upright off the floor where she fell.

At least the pain has subsided, Wendy thinks, as she prises her bloodshot eyes open. She sees panic etched across Jonathan's face, but doesn't feel one ounce of compassion for him. His delusion knows no bounds.

He laces her food with poison and then when she has a bad reaction, he is overcome with panic and concern for her wellbeing. She doesn't even feel pity for him; she doesn't believe it's his love for her that has made him deranged, more that it is his crushed ego, an ego that was always out of control.

"Are you alright?" Jonathan asks desperately, looking at her, "Can I get you some water?"

"I'm okay. Sorry, I don't know what came over me," Wendy replies, playing dumb.

"You're okay. Let's see if we can get you back onto your chair," he says as laughter erupts from the television as if to mock him.

"I think I'd like to take my shower now, if that's okay?"

"Yes, of course, I'll help you up," Jonathan replies.

Wendy struggles to get to her feet, which feel as if they have shards of glass sticking into them. She can feel the friction in her aching joints as they bend.

They seem to have completely lost their joint lubrication. Slowly and painfully, she manages to lift herself off the floor using the chair to help. Her captor helps to lift her, his roaming hands repulsing her clammy skin as they move across it. His hand strokes up her leg, feigning to steady it, but she isn't fooled, not for one second.

"Thank you," she tells him through gritted teeth when she is finally standing and taking her first step out of the prison, he has constructed especially for her.

Each and every step along the basement and toward the stairs is torture, and she is forced to accept her captor's steadying help. Her muscles feel torn apart with every movement, and her bones creak as if they might shatter into a million pieces at any moment.

The stairs are too narrow for Jonathan to help or steady her, but she accepts the pain and pulls herself up slowly, using the bannister to help her climb her mountain.

She knows he is close behind her; he always follows her up the stairs so he can stare at her exposed buttocks the short nightie fails to hide. The only thing driving her forward is the thought of hot water spraying onto her skin, running through her hair and relaxing her muscles, the only pleasure she now knows.

After an age, the long, arduous climb up through the house ends, and Wendy finally reaches the bathroom where she almost collapses onto the bathroom stool.

Jonathan follows her in, making a fuss, showing her the towels and fresh nightie he has already put out for her. He turns on the shower.

“Thank you,” she tells him.

“Take as long as you want; it'll make you feel better. I'll be in my bedroom if you need me.”

She thanks him again, but in her mind, she is begging for him to leave.

He does leave and pulls the bathroom door to, but leaves it ajar as he always does, since she was sick, telling her it's in case she needs him. She is thankful that he doesn't insist on staying in the bathroom with her, and that he at least gives her that much privacy.

Wendy uses the toilet and then hauls herself up to look at herself in the mirror above the sink, and is shocked at her awful state, even by her recent standards.

Her bloodshot eyeballs have sunk back further into their sockets, and the rings around them have darkened to the point that she looks as though she has two black eyes. The dull grey skin clinging to the bones of her gaunt face look like an old piece of leather, pockmarked with bruises and small thin red veins, a face she doesn't recognise. She is looking into the eyes of a stranger whose wispy thin hair is threatening to disappear entirely.

Wendy has to turn away from the ghoul in the mirror. It is too frightening and upsetting to look at any longer. Will

Jonathan not be happy until he has drained the life from her completely? Is that his aim, his revenge for her rejection?

Dragging the nightie over her head is a struggle in itself, and her shoulders burn as she manages to tug it off and drop it to the floor. The shower cubicle is already starting to steam up and she slides open the door, eager to feel the hot water on her tired skin.

A feeling of bliss washes over Wendy when she feels the soothing water.

Putting her head back into the flow intensifies the feeling, and for a moment, with her eyes closed, she almost forgets her plight. The feeling doesn't last, though. It can't, as the darkness begins to haunt her. She sees Brian, the man who became her rock, sitting on a chair in front of her. They are seated in the middle of Jonathan's kitchen, and he stands behind Brian with a large kitchen knife in his hand. Wendy tries to move, to go and help Brian, but she cannot get up from her chair. Her waist is tied to it.

"Phone her now, Wendy, or I will cut him," Jonathan orders, wielding the knife closer to Brian. "Tell your mother you will be gone for two to three months."

Wendy makes the phone call to her mum, doing as she is ordered.

She tells her mother that she is going travelling with Brian; anything to make Jonathan put the knife down. "Thank you, my love," Jonathan says when the call is over.

He then smiles at her as he pulls Brian's head back by his hair, bringing the knife down and across to slice Brian's throat open.

A scream almost escapes from deep inside Wendy as she relives the horror.

Brian's eyes bulge in terror as Jonathan's hand grabs his hair.

The thin red line the knife makes across Brian's neck opens up until it's gaping, the blood gushing out of the wound and streaming down Brian's chest to soak his entire body.

Wendy's eyes snap open to erase the vision, her body shaking in the hot water. She manages to stifle the scream, but cannot stop the sobs of sadness and despair trembling from within, her tears lost in the water flowing over her head.

"Are you nearly done?" a friendly but grotesque voice asks in Wendy's head.

She has no idea how long she has been standing here, sobbing under the hot water, and she has to pull herself together, quickly.

"Not yet. A few more minutes," she manages to reply.

"Okay, but not too much longer, please."

Wendy tries to concentrate on washing herself, and not thinking about Brian and the horror. She cannot help but wonder where Brian is now, however.

What did Jonathan do with his body?

Is he buried in the garden beyond the locked bathroom windows?

Does she really want to know?

Chapter 2

The bathroom mirror is completely steamed up when Wendy pulls her fresh nightie over her head. She doesn't wipe the condensation off it to take another look at herself before she leaves, as she really doesn't want to upset herself again. But thankfully, her body isn't aching as badly as it was. The hot water has eased her suffering somewhat.

Water vapour follows her out of the bathroom as she steps out.

In front of her, Jonathan is sitting on the end of his bed, his hands in his lap, waiting and watching the bathroom door like a daemon at the gates of hell.

"If showering were an Olympic sport, you would win the gold medal. I've always said that haven't I?" Jonathan jokes as he rises from his perch at the end of his bed.

"Yes, yes you have," Wendy agrees.

"Are you feeling better and refreshed?"

"Yes, thank you. The shower has helped."

"That's good. You had me worried for a minute there."

"I'm sorry, I didn't mean to," Wendy says nervously.

"It's okay. You can't help it if you're not feeling well," Jonathan replies sympathetically.

No, I can't, not when I'm being poisoned, by a sick fuck like you, Wendy thinks, but tries to smile at him.

"Let's get you back to your room, shall we? Maybe we could watch a bit more television before I have to work. Would you like that?"

"As long as you're not too busy?" Wendy says, not caring one way or the other.

"No, I'll be okay for a while."

Jonathan leads them down the first flight of stairs.

He is still nervous she may fall, so goes down just in front of Wendy.

"Could I have a cup of tea while we watch TV?" Wendy asks as they reach the ground floor, the kitchen opposite them.

"Yes, that's a nice idea," Jonathan says, heading into the kitchen. "You sit down while I make it."

Visions of Brian's throat being sliced open return to Wendy as she enters the kitchen and takes a seat while the tea is made.

The smell of cooking and tomato sauce lingers in the air to add to her torment.

Jonathan pulls open the cutlery drawer to get a spoon out, and Wendy wonders if that is where the knife used to kill Brian sits. A spoon in hand, he turns away from the drawer, leaving it open. Wendy imagines grabbing a knife while his back is turned, and slicing his throat open with it, or stabbing it into his back repeatedly—if only she had the strength to take him on. If she did have any strength left, she would, even if she died trying.

Anything to get out of this version of hell he has created especially for her.

"Shall we, then?" Jonathan asks, as if they are about to take a bike ride or a walk around the park. Wendy's legs strain to push her up from the chair and she shuffles out of the kitchen. By the time she reaches 'her room' and sits down, she is out of breath, her body shattered.

Jonathan follows her into her cage and puts her cup of tea down on the small table standing next to her chair, by the tall plastic jug of water and pile of books he 'kindly' provides for her. The books are her only solace once she is shut inside her dungeon. She has always enjoyed reading, but a book takes on a completely different importance when it is the only possible form of escape, for her mind at least.

Jonathan takes up his position on the couch to drink his tea. The television is still on from when they left for the shower, and a popular soap opera is currently showing. Jonathan would usually switch such a programme straight off, cursing the mindless rubbish.

To Wendy's surprise, however, he doesn't switch the TV over.

He just stares at the screen blankly, sipping his tea.

A commercial break interrupts the programme, filled with Christmas-themed adverts. Wendy calculates—by the amount of Christmas ads—that it must be at least late November, or could even be December.

She really is losing all track of time; she isn't even sure what month it is anymore.

Now, she has been captive in Jonathan's basement for over a month; she's almost sure of it. She wonders if her mother is concerned where she is? Jonathan has her phone, and she assumes that he is sending text messages to her from it, to delay her concerns. He is probably telling her mother what a good time she is having, and if her mother isn't concerned, there really isn't anyone else to wonder where she is, no one who would raise an alarm in any case.

Jonathan comes out of his stupor of staring at the television and gets up from the couch as the second set of commercials come on. He comes into her cage and picks up her empty mug and the jug, before taking them and putting them on his desk.

"Are you ready for bed?" he asks absently as he turns to walk back over.

"Yes, I'm ready," Wendy replies, not that she has any choice in the matter.

"Good, I'll just empty your bucket and get you some fresh water," he says. He closes her cage door and hooks the padlock onto it before he goes back upstairs with the bucket and jug.

He returns quickly with her bucket and jug and also leaves a treat for her, a small chocolate bar next to the pile of books.

"Goodnight Wendy. I'll be here all day tomorrow, so I'll see you in the morning."

"Okay, Jonathan," is all Wendy says as he pulls the bifold door across on the other side of her cage, shutting her in her tomb.

The sound of air squeezing between the seals of the door has become very familiar to Wendy, and as the light in her room fades, her anxiety rises and shadows darken and grow.

The small lamp she has, now her only source of light, is small and weak and hardly strong enough to aid with reading. Trying to stifle the sobs threatening to rise and burst from within her, she focuses her concentration on preparing herself for bed. The few small tasks that make up her routine are done quickly, though. Pouring a cup of water and picking up her book and chocolate only divert her concentration for a minute or two.

All too soon, Wendy is sitting in her small single bed, her book lying in her lap on top of the duvet in front of her. The book is the only possible means she has to transport herself out of her morbid surroundings, yet she does not move her hand to pick it up.

Her dark thoughts have ambushed her, coming to overwhelm her. The walls of her tiny room close in, threatening to crush the metal-framed bed into fragments, along with her mind, body, and soul. Dark shadows elongate and move as Wendy's vision loses its focus; they edge closer, ready to swallow her whole before the walls manage to crush her.

Tears stream down Wendy's cheeks, her despair dispelling the last morsels of hope she has been clinging onto for dear life. Images of Brian's kind and loving face swirl into view and Wendy clings to them for as long as she possibly can, before red, gushing blood contorts his terrified face, his gruesome neck gaping open. Her hands suddenly move to her chest to wipe away the thick sticky blood, but there is nothing there, only the dampness of her tears.

Her guilt for getting Brian involved almost matches her despair. Such a gentle man didn't deserve, and wasn't prepared for, Jonathan's wrath. Wendy had known that Jonathan's other side, his violent controlling tendencies driven by his jealousy, were frightening—tendencies that had grown stronger over the years, manifesting themselves more and more regularly.

Wendy had known the dangers and yet she had decided to—no, she had been forced to—confront them, and end their marriage and their relationship. She should have waited and not allowed Brian into her life, knowing Jonathan would find out about it.

As soon as the house was sold, that was when her new life far away from Jonathan was meant to have started, and now Brian had paid the ultimate, horrific price.

Gradually, Wendy's sobbing subsides, her exhausted, dilapidated body too weak to continue. Her heavy eyelids bring another escape from her torment and the pain in her joints, and her chin falls against her chest as sleep comes to blank out her misery, at least for a while.

Sweat pours from her as she sleeps with her back upright against the bed.

Her organs work desperately to counteract the chemicals she's ingested, but the more toxins her organs accept to process, the more they damage themselves.

Her skin tries to play its part by excreting the toxins straight out of her as sweat, but her pores are beginning to break down and disintegrate. Wendy's body is losing the battle it has been fighting against Jonathan's poison for far too long.

Jonathan Bradley is completely oblivious to the damage he is inflicting on his wife, who is the other side of the wall, opposite him. His deluded mind is trying to protect him from his humiliation which still clings to the fanciful and impossible reality that his medicine will cure his beloved wife of her treachery; he hopes his potion will convert her mind into loving him again and seeing them back together, to resume their blissful life.

No, Bradley's concentration is on his computer screen that reflects the images of pornography onto his spectacles, behind which his eyes bulge. His online research into new ways to improve and perfect his concoction for his wife doesn't last more than half an hour, however, his desires soon leading his concentration to wander away.

For two hours and more, Bradley sits in his man cave, satisfying himself, with barely a thought for Wendy. She is out of sight and out of mind, trapped, exactly where he wants her… for the time being, at least.

When he eventually clicks off the X-rated website, his business done, he considers going up to bed himself. After a stressful week at school with the brats and the extra pressure he is putting on himself looking after Wendy, he is shattered.

An early Saturday morning is inevitable; he must prepare Wendy's breakfast after all.

He doesn't move immediately though. His face stares blankly at the changing pictures of fabulous places around the world. His computer chooses to show them to him while it waits for him to click the mouse again. Slouched in the black leather executive chair and with a slack jaw, he imagines himself and Wendy visiting the places pictured on the screen.

She always wanted to travel to exciting and exotic destinations, having talked about it often, but why would he want to waste his hard-earned money holidaying in expensive and overrated holiday destinations?

She had worried him tonight when she collapsed, there is no doubt about that. Perhaps the dose he prescribed tonight was too big. Should he consider lowering it?

He must be more cautious if this therapy is going to be successful, he decides as he pushes himself out of the chair. The last thing he wants is to overdose his patient and kill her; he couldn't bear to lose Wendy and doesn't want to have to dispose of yet another body.

Looking back over his shoulder for one last time, Bradley takes a moment's pride in the invisible room he made with his own bare hands at the end of the basement.

His eyes glance over his workmanship, and even though he knows the door is there, he congratulates himself again at its camouflage; *the damn thing really is invisible*, he tells himself. It almost pains him when he switches the light off to leave it in darkness.

Wendy's electric lamp supply, is independent of the basement's lights, so she will continue to be able to enjoy her mountain of books for as long as she wants. She has always been an avid reader, and Bradley feels at ease as he climbs the stairs to get some well-deserved rest, safe in the knowledge that Wendy is settled in for the night.

Chapter 3

Far from being settled, Wendy's fight continues into the night. Her fatigue is no match for the pain of her sore limbs and the pounding in her throbbing head.

She has slept for a time, her brain shutting down to ease her miserable suffering, but her aching back has put pay to her release. Her spine seizes into its crooked sitting position where she fell to sleep, shooting excruciating pain into her swelling brain that forces her to wake.

Even if she can't hear the creaking of her back as she fights in agony to straighten it, she feels every horrendous crunch as she snaps the welds that have seized it up.

Almost crying out from the pain as she fights against the spasms to move down the bed and straighten her back, she eventually manages to ease herself flat.

Now, below her, the mattress is damp from the buckets of contaminated sweat her body has ejected out of her. Her skin has turned dry, almost crisp, her body running low on the water it needs to continue to recycle the chemicals. The dampness soaks against her body, cooling it quickly and causing her to shiver uncontrollably, jolting fresh pain through her unforgiving joints. A chattering noise escapes her mouth as her teeth vibrate together, the spasms having migrated to Wendy's jaw from the chill.

She manages to pull the duvet higher, up to her chin, in a futile attempt to warm herself, her body too weak to attempt anything more strenuous.

The thought of getting out of bed to try and sort herself out, is no more than a fantasy. She is stranded and the thought that she may never get out of bed again draws fear deep into her belly.

Time is something she has no control over, and it's all but irrelevant to Wendy now. Once her captor pulls her prison door across, the rest of the world is shut off from her.

There is no clock hanging on the wall to tell her the time, no window to show her the movement of the sun to at least tell her if it's night or day.

The only clue she receives is Jonathan's arrival, usually in the morning, and then again in the evening when he finishes work. She cannot even rely on that.

Sometimes, he doesn't arrive for either appointment, for reasons she can only imagine. Occasionally, he will tell her that he isn't going to be able to visit and will leave her extra supplies, or he just leaves the supplies in her cell and says nothing.

On other occasions, he just doesn't appear and only her gnawing hunger and thirst tell her he is overdue. She was once left for what she estimated were two or three days with no food or water, and he found her passed out on the bed when he did eventually arrive.

There was no apology or hint of explanation when he hauled her into a sitting position and put a cup of water to her mouth. Then, as soon as she was stable, he abandoned her again.

Maybe he thought she should be grateful that at least he had left her some extra food when he left, to make up for the meals she had missed?

After an unknown amount of time, the damp mattress begins to warm as it draws heat from Wendy's body, and thankfully, her shivering eases, despite her feet feeling like two blocks of ice. Her hands grip the top of the duvet, holding it close to her chin in fear it might somehow drop off the bed onto the floor, to leave her exposed.

A thought enters Wendy's mind as she lies in her tormented cocoon, her mind drifting in and out of consciousness, a thought that she cannot continue to exist like this. Jonathan is killing her in the slowest and most miserable way possible, but killing her nevertheless.

She has to start resisting Jonathan's heinous plans; if she is going to die, at least it can be on her own terms, to some degree anyway. She must stop trying to seem pleasant towards him, as it is getting her nowhere except closer to her death.

Could she refuse to eat his poisoned food, go on hunger strike, or would he just find another way to get his poison into her? What's to stop him injecting her? She certainly isn't strong enough to fight him off if he decides to inject her.

Perhaps start with small acts of resistance?

Stop pretending to be friendly, or give him the silent treatment to see how he reacts?

Wendy, drifting in and out of consciousness, not daring to attempt to move because it only brings pain, begins to develop her plans in the moments that she is alert. Plans are so easy to make in a dream state when you're half asleep, and the pieces of the jigsaw snap together so easily. The same plans that in the cold light of day sometimes don't fit together quite so readily.

Her grand plans drift away when sleep eventually comes to Wendy again, but she promises herself that her plans will not be forgotten as they develop.

Beads of sweat begin to form on Wendy's forehead while she sleeps, her body having discovered some reserves of water. She is unaware that they are there, and even when a solitary droplet runs down across her temple it doesn't disturb her. The first pangs of fresh pain don't wake her either, lost in the aching that already has hold of her body.

This new wave of agony grows quickly, though, and unstoppable, it courses out from her stomach like hot lava melting into every extremity of her long since battered carcass.

Now, Wendy does scream as her blood boils and her body contorts in agony before she suddenly goes completely rigid under her duvet.

The pain disfigures her face, her muscles taut, the scream bellowing out of her gaping mouth and flared nostrils. Her tongue, dry and hard, vibrates from the shockwave of her shriek that bounces off the walls of the enclosed cell, forcing its way out into the dark basement beyond. Precious fluid is drained from within Wendy to fill her eyes, tears streaming down both of her temples. This excruciating agony is totally unbearable, and it can mean only one thing.

Death flashes into Wendy's burning brain, her inevitable death that is upon her. Panic tries to override the impossible pain and then an unrelenting nausea bubbles up until Wendy jolts to the side, her creaking body throwing her head over the side of the bed.

Vomit erupts out of Wendy's cavernous mouth, deep red and black bile spraying into the thin gap between the bed and the wall beside it. The stream of sick flows out until her belly can tighten no more. The vile cascade momentarily stops, but only long enough to take a breath and for her belly to expand so that it can tighten again to force more of her gut onto the floor.

Her body racked in agony and her throat raw, Wendy prays for the vomiting to end so that she can fall back and collapse onto the bed. She doesn't care if her body is ridding itself of

Jonathan's poisonous food; the tortuous pain is too much to take.

Eventually, her stomach is empty of contents, and her continued retching produces nothing but more agony. Her brain repeatedly tells her stomach to stop its torture.

There is nothing left to come up and after one final retch—so deep that it threatens to eject her stomach lining out of her mouth—it ceases.

The episode over, Wendy does fall back onto the bed to try and regroup, but her suffering is not complete. Her poison-riddled body bursts into an uncontrollable fit, its fight for survival on a knife-edge. The bed below her shakes and rattles as her body jerks violently, the mattress not thick enough to absorb the onslaught. Each of her limbs fights against itself and her jaw bites down with so much pressure, it threatens to shatter her straining teeth.

Her back arches upwards, twisting unnaturally, one way and then the other as her limbs beat down. The muscles and ligaments in Wendy's neck tighten, protruding, ready to burst.

Bright twinkling stars zip across Wendy's vision, her brain paralysed, overloaded with shock and agony. The stars become brighter as darkness comes and Wendy's vision fades, as she tumbles into blackness and oblivion. With the darkness comes peace, and in an instant, her entire body goes limp and falls onto the mattress below her, motionless.

Chapter 4

Bradley stirs and turns over in his lovely warm bed. He has no idea what the time is, and he doesn't care since it is Saturday after all. He gets a satisfying weekend feeling, whilst deciding if he will stay where he is and snooze on for a while—no boisterous screaming children for him to have to deal with today.

Light piercing through even the tiniest gap in the curtains has brightened his bedroom enough to penetrate his eyelids and further stir him from his slumber. His brain starts to tick over and he knows that he will be fighting a losing battle if he thinks he is going to get any more sleep this morning. Nevertheless, Bradley doesn't open his eyes.

He gets himself as comfortable as possible and lets his mind wander for a while.

He considers what he will do for the day; he has to go shopping for groceries, unfortunately, but there is no rush to get that done. Maybe he will wash his car, but then again, maybe he won't.

He will decide later whether he feels up to it.

He wonders if Wendy is hungry and if she is awake yet.

He decided last night that he would give her a break from her medicine today. Following her turn yesterday, he has calculated that it's for the best in the long run.

An exciting idea then comes to him and his eyes pop open upon its arrival. Why doesn't he ride up to the town centre to get Wendy breakfast? He could surprise her with one of those overpriced trendy coffees that she used to enjoy so much, and a Danish pastry?

Stuff the expense, that's what he will do.

Perhaps he could even treat himself to a bacon sandwich while he is there.

Opening his curtains, Bradley sees that whilst the sun isn't as strong as it was yesterday, it is a pleasant enough morning and perfect for a ride into the town.

That is all the encouragement he needs, and he goes for a shower to get himself ready to go and get Wendy's surprise breakfast.

There is a chill in the air when Bradley sets off just after nine. The town centre is only a few minutes away, and although the roads are quiet—as is to be expected on a Saturday morning—Bradley decides to take the long route and ride through the park. Cruising through the park's gates, cruising being his top speed, he joins the few joggers and other cyclists out for their morning exercise. Unusually for Bradley, he leaves the Tarmac paths and takes his bike off-road for a change. The morning dew on the grass wets his tyres as he enjoys riding through the trees and rolling down the shallow slopes.

His fun is short-lived, as the park isn't big and he reaches the town gate in no time. Just as he is debating which direction to go when he exits, Bradley's phone starts to vibrate in his pocket, its ringtone quickly following the buzzing against his leg. Pulling on his brakes, he quickly fishes out the phone to see who is disturbing his enjoyment.

The screen indicates his twenty-one-year-old son's name flashing on his screen, and for a second, Bradley's thumb hovers over the red call reject button that is lit up beneath Matt's name. Huffing, Bradley swings his thumb over and taps the green answer button.

"Hello, son," Bradley answers in trepidation, wondering what hassle this call is going to cause him or how much it is going to *cost*.

"Hi Dad, how are you?"

"I'm well, just out on my bike to get some breakfast. How's life at uni?"

Matt is in his final year at Durham University, studying economics.

Bradley will be relieved when he's finished and starts paying his own bills instead of draining his father's bank account.

That's if he can ever find a job as yet another expert in economics.

"Busy and tough. The work and revision getting ready for next year's finals are building up. Isn't it raining there?"

"No, it's quite a nice morning. It's a bit chilly, but no rain."

"It's tipping down here. How's it going at school?"

"Oh, you know, same as it ever is, educating the stars of tomorrow," Bradley replies, sarcastically.

"They're lucky to be benefitting from your wealth of knowledge, Dad."

"They certainly are, son."

"And Wendy, have you spoken to her recently? Any change there?"

"No, Matt, I'm afraid not. I haven't spoken to her in a month or more," Bradley lies.

"Oh, that's a shame," Matt says with a tinge of sadness.

He was extremely close to Wendy, his stepmum. After all, she has been more like a second mother to him since he was twelve years old.

"One of those things, I'm afraid, Matt."

"I know Dad. It's just a shame though."

"Yes, I suppose it is," Bradley replies, trying not to sound too concerned and give anything away.

"Dad..."

Here it comes, Bradley thinks, *the real reason for the phone call.*

"Yes, Matt?"

"Have you any plans for Christmas? Mum's going away, and I've got too much uni work to catch up on over the holidays, so I was wondering if I can spend it with you?"

Bradley is hesitant with his answer while his brain calculates the bearing that Matt coming to stay might have on his situation with Wendy at his house.

The more he thinks about it, the more he panics... It could cause untold trouble.

"Yes, of course, you can come for Christmas, it'll be great to have you," Bradley replies, but what else could he say? He can't turn his son down, and if he did, it would look suspicious.

"Are you sure, Dad?"

"Yes, I'm sure. Sorry, you took me by surprise, that's all."

"Okay, brilliant. We can go out for a few drinks in the run-up, it'll be fun."

"It will be. When will you arrive?"

"Not sure yet. It'll probably next Thursday, the 20th, but I'll let you know for sure when I've booked my train ticket, okay?"

"Okay, that's fine. I'll look forward to it."

"Speak soon then, Dad."

"Okay, let me know."

Bradley lowers his phone from his ear and stays stood astride his bike for a time, while he contemplates how Matt coming for Christmas will affect his plans.

His heart races as his brain turns over, working out the implications.

Matt will arrive in just over a week's time, and before his arrival, the course of Wendy's therapy will have to come to a conclusion, one way or the other.

Wendy cannot be staying in her room in her current state when Matt arrives. That would be a recipe for disaster, there can be no doubt about that, Bradley decides.

Pushing forward, Bradley's legs start pedalling again slowly, almost too slowly to stay upright. He cycles out of the park gate, into the town, and before he knows it, he has arrived at the coffee shop without any recollection of the ride since Matt's phone call.

The shine has been taken off the day. He was looking forward to a day of rest and relaxation after deciding to pause Wendy's therapy for the day. Now, he is going to have to reconsider that decision. Can he afford any delays, or will he have to plough on, full steam ahead?

Oh, the hassle! Why can it never be straightforward? Bradley thinks as he leans his bike against the wall next to the coffee shop.

Wendy's breakfast is wrapped inside a paper carrier bag when he leaves the coffee shop. Bradley bought himself a Danish for breakfast too, but his appetite has gone, and he needs to get back anyway.

There is no time to stop again to get himself a bacon sandwich; things have changed.

"Hello, Mr Bradley," a female voice says as Bradley is about to pick up his bike off the wall, and he turns to see who is speaking to him.

A pretty young woman is dismounting her bike next to him, and his eyes fixate on her long slender legs that are bare beneath her shorts.

His eyes follow the legs down to her small white pumps and then start to move up again.

"Mr Bradley, are you okay?"

"Yes, sorry, do I know you?"

Bradley raises his eyes quickly to her face, suddenly realising he is staring at her legs.

"It's Emma, Mr Bradley, I was in your class a couple of years ago. I'm at college now."

"Yes, Emma, of course, I remember," he lies. "How are you and how is college?" Bradley asks, his eyes glancing back down to Emma's legs.

"It's great. I've made lots of new friends. I'm studying biology so that I can hopefully go on and study veterinary medicine at university. It's not easy, is it?"

"No, it can be quite complicated," Bradley replies, now looking into Emma's beautiful blue eyes.

"I know, but you seem to know everything there is to know about biology."

Is she flirting with me? Bradley suddenly thinks, his crotch stirring, *perhaps she might like to come back to mine for some 'extra' lessons?*

"Well, there isn't much I don't know about biology. I live close by and would happily go over anything you're not sure of. I'm free now?" he says seeing his way in with this gorgeous young woman, already stripping her off in his mind.

"That's very nice of you, Mr Bradley, and if you weren't such a miserable old git who bullies his students, I might have taken you up on that!" Emma says, getting back on her bike and starting to ride off. "Bye, Mr Bradley," she says, smiling and waving.

Bradley is flabbergasted, speechless for a moment. And then his face starts to redden and his anger boils up. He is about to blow. Emma is already too far away and by the time his anger peaks, it's too late. She has turned the corner and gone. 'Fucking bitch', he says to himself as he trembles with anger at the side of the street.

Grabbing his bike off the wall, for a second, he contemplates pedalling after the jumped-up little slag and teaching her a lesson. His fists whiten on the bike's handlebar grips, his rage frothing. *If I ever see her again*, he thinks as he turns and rides for home.

Bradley's anger rumbles on as he rides directly back to his house, but he doesn't go for the scenic route through the park. He woke up this morning in a good mood, decided to come and get Wendy a surprise breakfast, and how is he repaid? With a fucking phone call from his son to foul up his plans, and an altercation in the street with a bitch of an ex-student.

Why do these things happen to me, he thinks, *what have I done to deserve them? They'll all be laughing on the other side of their faces one day,* he tells himself.

Slamming the front door behind him, Bradley takes the breakfast bag into the kitchen and puts it down on the side. His hands grab the side of the work surface, his breathing heavy as he continues to wonder why people can't just leave him alone to get on with his life. He leans forward, bowing his head, his arms outstretched onto the work surface, trying to get some blood back into his dizzy head and to calm down.

Eventually, his breathing slows and his anger subsides.

He doesn't want Wendy to see him angry and upset; it could undo the good work they have already done together and slow her progress. She needs to see him calm and friendly, see how he really is, the man with whom she fell in love.

Bradley is convinced that she is close to remembering and falling back in love with him. She has been so calm and friendly with him recently, a completely different person than when she started her treatment.

She was angry and vile towards him then, and even violent on occasion.

It pained him to do it, but he had to beat that out of her in the early days of her therapy.

With perseverance, it will be tight, but this could all be settled by the time Matt is due to arrive. He and Wendy could be happy again by then and living back in their house together. She would love to see Matt, he is sure of that; they were very close and to spend Christmas together, how exciting would that be for her?

Should he tell Wendy of Matt's visit for Christmas? Perhaps it will help speed her through her treatment. Perhaps his phone call was a blessing in disguise?

No, he tells himself, *don't get carried away with yourself*. Giving her that information is going to have to be considered, written into her therapy schedule if it is appropriate after some considerable research. For now, he will keep that information to himself, but it has put a completely different slant on Matt's request. Bradley is looking forward to his arrival now.

Invigorated, Bradley picks up the breakfast bag off the worktop, suddenly eager to see his beloved wife. He turns and carries the bag out into the hallway and toward the basement door.

Chapter 5

A rank smell wafts out of Wendy's room when Bradley pulls the door across, a smell he hasn't encountered before, when opening up Wendy's room. Worry and dread hit him before he even looks beyond the wire mesh, and when he does, his worry turns into panic.

"Wendy," he calls as he rushes to unlock the padlock on the cage's door.

Wendy's face, poking out from beneath her duvet, is a deep shade of grey and she is completely motionless. He can't even see a sign of her breathing.

The pungent stink makes Bradley gag as he rips the door open and rushes into the room.

Wendy doesn't stir an inch, and the smell, *oh my god the smell*, Bradley thinks as he pushes through it towards his wife, his *dead* wife.

What have you done, Bradley scolds himself, *you have killed your beautiful wife! What kind of monster are you? You were supposed to be helping her, treating her, but you went over the top, gave her too much medicine and killed her, you fucking evil monster!*

For a moment, Bradley stands at the end of the bed, looking down at Wendy's macabre face, grief-stricken and almost afraid to go near her. His heart racing and his eyes welling up, he is lost, wondering what to do next. How could this have happened?

He had been extremely careful measuring the doses that he had mixed into Wendy's medicine. Some of the ingredients were toxic, even deadly in some doses, but he had diluted those chemicals to safe levels—even if he wasn't one hundred percent positive how the chemicals would react together.

So confident is he that he took all the safety precautions necessary, he starts to think of what else could have caused this failure in Wendy's treatment. His demented mind begins to shift the blame, unwilling to accept the responsibility for this catastrophe.

Perhaps Wendy had an unfortunate underlying health condition that he was unaware of and couldn't account for. Or, maybe she had an unforeseeable allergic reaction to one of the ingredients in her medicine? How could he have accounted for either possibility?

His calculations and research had been exacting, but no experimental treatment is guaranteed to succeed, especially when the patient has an underlying condition or weakness.

The burden of guilt begins to lift from Bradley's twisted mind and his head starts to clear. He has to accept that the experiment is concluded and that in this instance, the results are not favourable. An unfortunate result indeed, but one that in this case, couldn't have been avoided.

The only thing to do now is wrap up the failed experiment and go back to the drawing board. He is confident that his basic theory is sound, if not perfect, but there is no reason he cannot improve his treatment, or even perfect it.

He has done the hard work. He has built the required controlled environment in which he is standing and it would be a shame to let his endeavours up to this point go to waste.

He needs to regroup, go over his research, fine-tune his calculations… and begin again.

The subject of his next treatment could be a problem, but one that is not insurmountable. There is one improvement that comes to mind immediately in regard to the subject, and it seems obvious to him now. He has been foolish and sentimental with his last subject, Wendy. He needs to acquire a younger, fitter subject to give the treatment the best chance of success, and he already has an ideal candidate in mind, the lovely Emma.

Everything happens for a reason, and his bike ride this morning proves that point.

Yes, he thinks, she will be the perfect candidate. Young, beautifully fit, and feisty too. Her rudeness towards him earlier will make for a very interesting subject. She will certainly be challenging, and if the treatment is successful, the rewards will be extraordinary.

Bradley's desire surges at the very thought of taking Emma on as his new subject.

Her soft but firm skin will feel like silk under his touch. The image of Emma's bare firm legs fills his thoughts and drives Bradley to move and get his preparations underway. His first task, though, is to deal with his last subject, Wendy.

Bradley's delusion hasn't left him completely emotionless. It is with a heavy heart that he looks at his wife again, debating on the best course of action to take with her.

He moves to the other side of the room, looking at the task ahead of him.

He sees the floor beside Wendy's bed and is shocked to see the mess she has made. The floor confuses him for a moment; it is covered in a thick black sludge which has also splattered onto the lower part of the wall, and he leans in lower to take a closer look.

Bradley's gagging returns as he finds the source of the disgusting smell that is hanging in the air. He backs away from the putrid substance as the realisation of what it is hits him.

He congratulates himself on having the foresight to lay lino flooring in this part of the basement, as it will make it a lot easier to clean up the mountains of vomit from the floor.

Wendy was obviously very ill in the night.

Her weak body must have been overcome and given up.

He will have to move the bed to get to the mess, and the floor and wall will have to be cleaned thoroughly before his next guest arrives to take up residence.

He cannot afford any cross-contamination between subjects.

The question, therefore, is what to do with Wendy, and it's a question he doesn't have an answer for immediately.

She deserves to be treated with respect, and he'll be damned if he is going to chop up her body and bury it under the flower bed in the garden, as he did with Brian. That was all that arsehole deserved, but his beloved wife is different, he will not bury her next to him.

Looking down at Wendy's peaceful but morbid face, Bradley decides to put off making the decision on what to do with her. He sombrely pulls her duvet cover up to cover her face and then begins to tuck it in around her sides.

He rolls her onto her side one way, to make sure the duvet covers her back, and then rolls her the other to ensure she is tightly packed inside.

With Wendy entombed in the duvet cover, Bradley leans down and scoops his arms under her body to pick her up off the bed. He prepares himself for the heavy lift and then takes the strain. His back and arms easily lift Wendy's body off the bed and he surprises himself with his strength. He doesn't acknowledge that his wife is emaciated and a fraction of the weight she should be, a result of the torture he has inflicted unwaveringly upon her.

God forbid he would take responsibility for his actions towards his estranged wife.

Bradley squeezes his load through the cage's door and walks over to the floor beside his couch, and gently lowers Wendy down onto the basement floor.

He debates whether to put her onto the couch but decides against it.

He will want to sit down and watch TV at some point, after all.

With Wendy out of the way, Bradley strips the bed and lifts the frame out of the way.

He then goes upstairs, puts the bedclothes into the washing machine and gets the cleaning products he needs. Returning to the basement, he goes about cleaning up Wendy's mess before giving the whole room a thorough clean down.

The whole cleaning process doesn't take long, even though Bradley retches a few times behind his facemask when removing the vomit. He uses a shovel to scrape up the majority of the thick, dark red gooey substance that he can barely look at. Wendy's toilet bucket, into which he drops the vomit, has some weight to it when he carries it upstairs to dispose of.

By the time he has finished, he has built up quite a hunger and remembers the pastries in the breakfast bag sitting on his desk. The coffee has long since gone cold, so he goes to make himself a nice hot mug of tea that he can drink whilst consuming the pastry-laden cakes.

Bradley sets himself up in front of his computer so that he can do some research whilst he eats. There is no time like the present. As soon as the computer has started up, he opens a search page and types *Emma* into the search bar. Of course, nothing relevant comes up from just typing in Emma, but he has more to go on than just her first name. He knows where she lives, what school she went to and can guess which college she is attending.

Bradley is licking the last few crumbs of pastry and sugar from his fingers when some promising search results start being presented on the screen in front of him.

By the time he has finished his tea too, Bradley has got to know Emma pretty well. He finds it amazing what information some people will upload to the internet for the world to see.

Even though he gets distracted for quite some time browsing through the pictures Emma has seen fit to upload of herself for him—some of which are quite revealing—he soon has some very solid information on the poor girl.

For instance, somebody has kindly taken pictures of Emma posing on her bicycle and in her prom dress on prom night, outside the same house. Bradley is familiar with the roads and byroads within Lemsfield, and quickly recognises the road in the background of the pictures; he even thinks he has seen the house. Emma's house.

He also discovers that she plays badminton at Lemsfield Leisure Centre.

There are lots of pictures of her playing for the local team, and excitingly, a video showing her running around in her short gym skirt that Bradley enjoys watching more than once.

Always thorough, Bradley right-clicks his mouse so that he can check the date stamps on the pictures of Emma playing badminton. The dates the pictures were taken is provided, and interestingly, so is the time.

The majority were taken between the hours of 6 p.m. and 7 p.m., and a quick check of his calendar tells Bradley that the dates were all Saturdays.

Pleased with himself, Bradley leans back in his chair, his arms stretching back and above his head. Within half an hour, he has discovered where Emma lives and where she will be between six and seven on a Saturday night—where she will be tonight.

He feels as though he has got to know her very well, intimately, and the more he sees, the more he likes. He has already decided that Emma will be the perfect subject to continue his treatment, and he is confident that this time, it will be a resounding success.

A swarm of butterflies swirl in Bradley's stomach when a thought enters his head. He trembles with nerves as the thought develops and morphs into an action plan.

His desire overrides any considerations of caution, his unhinged mind placating the obvious dangers of moving forward so quickly.

He has to see Emma tonight, in the flesh.

His feelings for her have grown ridiculously strong in the short time since the original thought of taking her on as his new subject popped into his head less than two hours ago.

What is the harm of taking a trip to the leisure centre to see her arrive for her badminton session? He may even be able to sit discreetly somewhere and watch her play a game or two.

He also knows the route home she will probably take if she is riding her bike, and if the opportunity arises to take her under his wing, then why wait unnecessarily to begin her transformation?

Bradley's eyes slowly close as he sits and fantasises about the possibility of Emma taking up residence in her new room, just a few feet away from where he is.

He envisages her tender young skin beneath the silk nightie she will surely wear for him as she lies on top of her bed that he has prepared for her.

He knows her treatment won't be easy, he isn't stupid, but nothing worthwhile is, and Matt's arrival for Christmas will have to be carefully planned and accounted for. Bradley has already taken that into consideration.

The basement will be turned from a man cave—where Matt might like to spend time—into a storage room that will not be of interest to him and that he will have no reason to go into. Matt will be staying for a week or more, and other challenges will need to be overcome.

Bradley is sure, however, that Matt will not want to spend that much time at home with his boring old dad and there will be plenty of opportunities to continue with Emma's care.

Emma will also have to be kept under a certain amount of sedation for the duration of Matt's stay, so that she is kept in a docile state.

Emma banging around in her room while Matt is staying cannot be allowed to happen.

Bradley's head is spinning with all the different connotations of moving Emma into her new room, having her stay, and starting her treatment therapy.

All of which is only exasperated by Matt's planned visit.

No matter how complicated Bradley's latest endeavour may appear and how many moving parts there are, it pales into insignificance compared to his growing excitement. His eagerness to get underway is unrivalled. While his anticipation to see Wendy settled in was profound, it pales in comparison to the excitement and nervousness he is experiencing now.

Bradley pushes on the arms of his executive chair to get to his feet and wanders over to Wendy's discarded body, rolled up in the duvet cover on the floor.

Don't be jealous, my love. You will always be the one, Bradley's inner voice tells his unfortunate wife as he looks down upon her. *I'm sorry that it didn't work out for you, but life moves on and I'm sure you would want me to be happy.*

All he can see of Wendy's body is the hair on the top of her head, a section of her forehead that pokes out of the end of the rolled duvet, and the top of her toes at the other.

A genuine feeling of sadness comes over Bradley at the loss of his wife, a feeling that he doesn't care for. *Stop wallowing*, he tells himself, *preparations need to be made,* and his excitement returns as he turns away to get on with the task at hand.

Chapter 6

Placing the last item that he has calculated he could possibly need tonight into his carry case, Bradley slowly pulls the zip across to close his trusty bag. The baseball cap sitting on his head feels alien to him, as he never wears a hat apart from on special occasions.

Actually, his whole outfit makes him feel uncomfortable, dressed in joggers and pumps, with a scarf wrapped around his neck under the hoodie. He feels like a yobbish youth about to go out to terrorise the local population for the evening.

His hands rest on top of his well-used bag and he takes a moment to consider what might happen tonight. *This is only a reconnaissance expedition*, he tells himself, *to see how the land lies, to get a feel for Emma's routine*. Yet, he knows full well that he will return home disappointed if that is all that happens tonight.

If the opportunity presents itself, which subconsciously he is banking on, his young and gorgeous new subject, Emma, will by lying in her bed before the night is out, for him to admire.

You are moving way too fast, an annoying voice in his head tells him. *You are taking too much of a risk if you try anything tonight!*

The nagging voice is right and Bradley knows it, as his nerves tell him the exact same.

Wendy's abduction happened almost by accident. Bradley had invited her round to his house under the false pretence of discussing their separation and divorce, when the actual reason was to plead with her to reconsider leaving him.

He hadn't planned to abduct her that day.

It was supposed to be a last resort if there was no changing her mind.

Nothing was going to happen on that night as it was too perilous; she could have told anyone she was coming to see him, and she *had* told someone. She had told Brian.

Brian drove Wendy the short distance from her house to Bradley's.

Hiding in the shadows of the bedroom window, Bradley saw them pull up a short distance away and Wendy get out of the car. Brian didn't drive off when Wendy left the car, rather he stayed there parked on the kerb, to wait for her.

As soon as Wendy entered the house, Bradley lost his temper and demanded that Wendy tell Brian to leave so that they could talk properly without him hanging around.

Wendy refused, trying to stand up to Bradley... She should have known better.

Bradley, in a fit of rage, manhandled Wendy, wrestled her phone off her and rang Brian himself, and in no uncertain terms told Brian to leave. But far from leaving and to Brian's credit, moments later, he was knocking on Bradley's front door, worried for Wendy's safety.

The rest, as they say, is history; suffice to say Bradley had to adapt to the unexpected situation. Brian was killed and Wendy was trapped.

All Bradley had to do was cover his tracks and get rid of Brian's car.

Emma is different. There is no inviting her round, he's already tried that. Bradley is going to have to kidnap her off the street, as what other way is there? He was prepared to do that with Wendy and that had filled him with trepidation, and now he is going to do it with Emma, an outsider, his nerves are beginning to fray.

Bradley looks at his wristwatch.

It is time to leave if he is going to get into position at the leisure centre to witness Emma's arrival at her badminton session. His lust overrides any notion of putting tonight off, even though he can think of several good reasons. It is exhausting, all this planning and scheming. He is already weary from what Wendy has put him through today and taking care of Emma will be a further burden, but one that will bear fruit, he is sure of it.

With no pain, comes no gain, Bradley thinks as he dips his baseball cap on his head slightly and picks up his carry case. Pulling closed his front door gently, Bradley scans his road in each direction, in case he is being watched.

Paranoia is good, he tells himself. It will keep you alert, cautious, and therefore safe.

Darkness has already fallen, which is to his advantage.

The new energy-saving streetlights that have recently been installed are worse than the old ones. They hardly light up the street directly below them, never mind offering to light up the front of his house, again to his advantage.

Bradley casually moves around to the side of his car, a classic, just like his bicycle. He swiftly opens the driver's door the old-fashioned way, with the key, and swoops into the driver's seat before he can be noticed. The engine doesn't rush itself, but it starts the first time and he looks over his shoulder to pull the long body of the car off his drive.

He doesn't see a single soul from the time he leaves his house to when he drives off along his road. So far, so good. Bradley's arm moves into its favoured position for driving, resting on the driver windowsill, hand on top of the wheel.

The car may not be flash or modern, but it has a certain style to it and it is extremely versatile. With the back seats down, the long body will fit an inordinate amount of stuff into it; there was no need to hire a van when he was forced to move out of his house.

These little city cars are all well and good, but Bradley often wonders what these people do when they have to move anything more than their groceries. *They ask people like me with a proper car for help, that's what they do! Bleeding pain in the arses, the lot of them.*

In less than ten minutes, Bradley is swinging the nose of his car into the entrance of the leisure centre. The car park is bustling, all the fitness freaks out in force, dressed in their own particular form of fashion as if they were on their way to compete at the Olympics.

Most couldn't run up their own stairs Bradley decides, but at least they look the part.

Driving to the front of the large car park, Bradley needs to find a parking space with a good view of the main entrance and the bike rack next to it if he is going to get a worthwhile look at Emma.

The fitness freaks have taken up the prime position at the front, however, to save themselves walking too far. *Oh, the irony*, Bradley thinks and pulls up to wait for a space to become free. He has plenty of time until he expects Emma to arrive. He made sure of that.

The wait isn't long, and a man in a full tracksuit complete with matching headband and sports bag emerges from the main door, gets into his car, and vacates an ideal space.

Pulling forward quickly so as not to miss his opportunity, Bradley carefully reverses back until he is perfectly positioned right opposite the bike rack and the entrance. Now, it is a waiting game and Bradley is prepared to wait. It adds to his excitement.

While he waits, Bradley turns on his phone's camera and positions the phone onto the dashboard in front of him, its lens aimed out of the windscreen, towards its objective. It takes him a minute of fiddling to get the phone balanced, and until he is satisfied that the cameras lens is angled to get the best shot of the bike rack and entrance.

Once Emma arrives, he intends to press record and then leave the phone to film her arrival. That will allow him to concentrate on Emma, as he doesn't want to watch her through a lens.

He wants to enjoy her with his own eyes.

The video will be a backup, something he can watch later if he doesn't manage to find the opportunity to take her back to her new room tonight.

Minutes pass, and with each second that ticks by, Bradley's anticipation grows. There is no guarantee that Emma will be on her bike when she arrives, as her parents might be driving her to her session tonight. But there is also no guarantee that she is coming at all.

Bradley can feel it in his bones that she is on her way, that she draws nearer with every passing second, and his neck starts to ache from swivelling his head around at any sign of movement, a curse escaping his lips with each disappointment.

As the time draws closer to six, Bradley's frustration builds.

Has he got it all completely wrong, and did he look at the calendar correctly? He is sure about the time. It is clearly stated if you know where to look on each image, as is the date, but only the date is given, not the day. Perhaps he made a mistake?

Or did Emma arrive before him?

Is she already inside? Surely not, as he arrived well before her session was due to start. Should he risk getting out of the car to investigate?

Perhaps he could see in through a window?

Bradley's hand wipes his brow, his mixed feelings getting the better of him.

Then, just as Bradley is trying to work out his next move, a female cyclist zips into view before braking sharply at the bicycle stand, straight ahead of him.

Bradley jumps into action before he has even determined if the female is Emma. He needs to start recording. In his rush to press the right button on his phone, he knocks it completely over, his pernickety placement of the device blown. "Motherfucker," he curses as he swipes his hand across the dashboard, his anger getting the better of him and sending the phone spinning across the dash before it tumbles into the passenger footwell.

Calm down man, he tells himself, *this isn't the time to lose your shit*.

His phone forgotten, Bradley stares out of the windscreen, begging to get a good look at the woman hastily locking up her bike.

He focuses on the new arrival, who unfortunately has her legs covered by tracksuit bottoms but does have long blonde hair, just like Emma's. *It must be her*, he tells himself as he prepares for her to rise from locking her bike so that he can see for sure. *She's just running late*.

Raindrops hit the windscreen just as the woman finishes fiddling with her lock. And not just a few drops, either; they immediately distort Bradley's view. His hand quickly swipes the wiper stalk in front of him, but nothing happens, as his ignition is off. "Bloody hell!" he shouts at the top of his voice as his hand drops to fumble with the ignition keys, and the woman runs towards the entrance of the leisure centre to get out of the rain.

The wipers crawl across the windscreen just in time to show Bradley the woman's back disappear inside. His anger boils over, sticking in his throat, and all he can do is slam his hand onto the steering wheel in front of him. Bradley's simmering anger nearly turns into tears as his head bows to rest with a thump onto the wheel, his breathing heavy.

The rain taps onto the roof of the car as it would a tin roof. Soundproofing wasn't top of the list when this vehicle was designed. Bradley brings his breathing under control. *It's just a setback, insignificant in the greater scheme of things,* he tells himself.

Straightening his back, Bradley knows that he has to keep his temper under control if his task is going to be completed successfully.

He might have lost this battle but it has steeled his determination to get his just desserts.

Bradley again considers getting out of the car to sneak a glimpse of Emma, but decides against it. The consequences of anybody seeing him loitering about like a dirty old man would be dire, and the thought he had earlier of going inside to watch her play, he realises was ridiculous. Patience is the name of the game. He will relax for a while, stay put and wait for his prize to emerge from her game.

Let her play, he thinks, *let Emma enhance her fitness even further for me.* Calmness returns and Bradley leans over to fish his phone out of the footwell where it landed. He might as well use the time constructively and study the route she is most likely to take on her way home.

Almost sure of which way Emma will ride home, Bradley closes his phone to allow his eyes to adjust to the darkness in plenty of time before Emma is due to finish her session.

He turns and leans over to the back seats, to release the catches and drop the seats down. He admires the open space now afforded by the back of the car, which is enough to slide a coffin into if he so decides.

The rain has increased its tap on the car's roof. Now, it's coming down heavily and set in for the night, Bradley reckons. His first thought is that the rain is a curse, but he now sees that is quite wrong, as it's a blessing in disguise for him tonight. Not only will it provide him cover to complement the darkness, but it will also hamper Emma's ride home, whilst also emptying the streets of nosey busybodies who may see something they shouldn't.

Spirits lifted, Bradley allows his excitement to return, accompanied by anticipation as he notices that far from the time dragging, it has flown by, and Emma's hour is nearly up.

There will be no hurried mistakes this time.

His phone is in his pocket, and there is no videoing to distract him.

His attention will be entirely on Emma when she comes out to collect her bike.

With the time approaching five to seven, Bradley starts his engine to let his wipers clear his view. His nerves start to jangle, and he fidgets in his seat while he waits for the last few minutes that seems to take longer than the last hour, to pass.

The clock time on his dash reaches seven and then slowly slips past it.

Anytime now, Bradley thinks, *give her time to finish up and say her goodbyes*. A shadow crosses the main door and Bradley's hands move to his steering wheel, squeezing it tightly. The glass doors slide open, allowing someone to leave, and it's a young girl.

He sees that almost immediately, but this girl has brown hair, not Emma's blonde locks.

A car pulls up outside the entrance, blocking Bradley's view, a parent picking up their precious child, no doubt. "Move it, arsehole," Bradley says to himself, panicked that his opportunity to see Emma is about to go horribly wrong again. More girls appear from behind the car, all scattering out into the car park. However, none are going for the bike rack. Then as quickly as it arrived, the car is gone, relieving Bradley of some of his tension.

Over the next few minutes, other girls appear from inside and then just as quickly they disappear into the night. Three or four retrieve their bikes from the rack, but none are Emma unless he's missed her somehow. Some have their hoods up.

No, the bike Emma arrived on is still in position, Bradley assures himself. *What if that wasn't Emma? You're assuming it was, but you can't be sure*. Bradley starts to worry.

The trickle of girls exiting the leisure centre slows until it comes to a complete stop, and now Bradley really starts to panic.

Was that Emma arriving, and *is she even here*? his mind asks.

The entrance doors slide open and Bradley's heart jumps in his chest. Emma steps into the open doorway like a mirage, no mistaking her long blonde hair and pretty face.

She doesn't rush out into the rain, but stands just inside the entrance, looking at the downpour falling from the night sky.

Emma doesn't pull a face, only smiles as if it will be a fun adventure to ride home in the wet. Then she zips up her coat and pulls her hood over her head. Bradley is transfixed by the vision standing in the doorway; her beauty is undeniable. She will make for a perfect subject.

Her hood up, Emma makes her dash for the bike rack, which has a roof fitted over it and she bends to reach her lock. Bradley is so mesmerised by watching Emma that he nearly forgets to follow her out of the car park as she begins her ride, but he does follow.

He is so nervous as he follows Emma, that he missed his first gear change completely, crunching the car's gearbox into second just in time to stop again at the car park's entrance.

Emma doesn't stop.

She rolls out and onto the road, turning in the direction Bradley anticipates.

Stationary, just back from the road, Bradley pauses and watches as Emma rides off into the darkness, her red backlight glowing in the pouring rain. Bradley is in no rush to drive off to follow her, as much as he is tempted. He is sure she will be on this road for a fair distance yet, and there is no point racing off down the road after her, hounding her and giving the game away. This part of town is too busy.

There are quieter and more secluded roads ahead on Emma's journey.

Eventually, when he can resist no more, Bradley pulls out into the road.

He doesn't accelerate too hard, taking it steady, his eyes searching immediately for any sign of a glowing red light in the rain ahead.

Bradley travels farther than he had planned and there is still no sign of Emma's rear backlight. *Don't panic*, he tells himself, *she must be just ahead*, and then he sees a tell-tale dim red glow in the distance. Emma, surprisingly, is already approaching the large bend in the road that leads onto the quieter roads on this side of the city. They could nearly be described as country roads. Bradley closes in some, but not too much, as he doesn't want to crowd her. Not yet, at least. He expects Emma's light to start arcing away as she rides around the bend, but it doesn't. It carries straight on and then suddenly disappears completely.

"NO!" Bradley shouts in shocked confusion.

She has to use this road to get to her house, where the fuck has she gone? His mind despairs.

It suddenly dawns on him where Emma has vanished to. How could he have been so stupid? She has taken the route through the park and the woods, a much shorter route for someone on a bike. Did he assume that she wouldn't go that way at night because it would be too scary for her? Well if he did, he was wrong; she obviously doesn't scare that easily.

The park and the woods have multiple exits.

Think which one she will use, Bradley challenges himself.

His foot floors the accelerator, a very rare occurrence for Bradley, especially in the wet, and the car lurches forward. If Emma is going straight home, there is only one exit for her to use, the main one at the back of the woods. No matter how brave she is, in this wet darkness, it's her only option, the only path through that is completely tarmacked and lit up at night.

All the others are no more than walking paths, with no lights to guide her way, and too treacherous for her to attempt.

With his car swerving around the long bend in the road, Bradley has already decided that this will be his chance to snatch Emma. He will arrive on the other side of the woods before she has ridden that distance, and provided there is no one else around, it will be the perfect opportunity to surprise

Emma as she emerges. The exit is small, on a quiet stretch of road with plenty of overgrown bushes and trees to offer cover.

Indicating right, Bradley has reached the turn for the road that backs onto the woods in no time. He knows exactly where the exit is located on this quiet little road since he has ridden out of it himself many a time. After his turn, on the car's right-hand side, the dark and foreboding woods loom. It's only a relatively small wood, but it gives Bradley the creeps and he feels an admiration for Emma for having the guts to ride through alone at night.

Who knows what could be lurking in them?

Seeing the exit, which is no more than a hole in the surrounding bushes and trees, Bradley drives past it to park up. As he goes by, he looks into the ominous black hole to see if there is any sign of Emma's bicycle lights, but he doesn't see any. Only the weak light emitted from the path's street lamps.

Bradley hasn't much time. Emma can't be far behind him and he needs to be in position and ready. He grabs his bag from the passenger seat and rushes to open it. He picks out the syringe that he has prepared especially for Emma and holds it up to the light to double-check it. The syringe will help Emma through her transition and will keep her docile for the trip home. Bradley is not an expert in prescribing morphine. He used it on occasions with Wendy, but only in small doses when he had 'things' he needed to do with her.

This syringe has a larger dose sitting inside it, which should be enough to incapacitate Emma for long enough to get her settled. If only it were as easy as they show in the movies, using an old rag with a splash of chloroform to incapacitate your subject.

Unfortunately, that is Hollywood magic and doesn't work in the real world.

With the syringe in his fist and butterflies in his belly, Bradley opens the car door and gets out. *This is it*, he tells himself as he pulls the scarf that sits around his neck up over his nose and repositions his cap lower down on his head.

His body feels weak and frightened, unwilling to participate in his sordid scheme. His head overpowers his body's misgivings and forces it to comply, and then Bradley is in position behind the foliage at the very edge of the exit.

From his vantage point, he can see through the branches and leaves into the woods beyond and straight up the dimly lit path that Bradley is counting on Emma using. The rain has eased off a small amount, but it's still coming down and doing its job.

There is no sign of anyone around to disturb Emma's arrival.

Bradley ignores the drops of water dripping from the peak of his baseball cap, his eyes and his concentration fixed on the path where it winds into view a short distance away. The wind moves the foliage back and forth in front of his vision but it is of no consequence, and Bradley's stomach burns when he sees a bicycle light appear out of the darkness.

The burning sensation spreads down into his legs and out into his arms; he has never been so scared in his life as he is in this moment, as Emma pedals closer.

Now, Bradley's brain tells his body when Emma is about to breach the exit of the park. He doesn't feel his body move but it has.

It has stepped out across the entrance just in time for Emma's arrival.

Emma sees the silhouette as it moves across the narrow exit instantaneously, and panic sets in. She has used all of her concentration to ride through the park in the darkness and the rain, she has needed it not to fall off the path and end up in a heap in the bushes. She pulls her brakes, but they are wet and they're not going to stop her in time. She is going to collide with the poor person who has just entered the park unless she takes evasive action.

Swerving to avoid hitting the person, her front wheel strays off the tarmacked path and onto the soaked grass, where it loses all traction. The bike's front wheel slides from under Emma and she is falling, but at least she has missed the person, she thinks as she hits the ground.

Luckily, the wet grass is soft and she slides across it, coming to a stop quickly, her bike in a heap beside her. Stunned for a moment, Emma lies on her back, looking up at the treetops and the rain falling towards her that sparkles in the light of the lamp above.

Regaining her wits, she decides that she hasn't hurt herself, not seriously anyway. There are no broken bones, thankfully. She pushes herself up onto her elbows to see if her bike is damaged and to check that she hasn't frightened the other person to death.

The silhouette of the other person is coming over in her direction, presumably to check if she is okay. "I'm fine," Emma says as they approach, the grass beneath her squelching when she tries to sit up. "Sorry about that, I didn't see you until the last second."

The shadowed person says nothing in reply as they bend over to help Emma up. "It's okay, I can manage thank you," Emma tells them as a hand grips onto her arm.

A sharp pain stabs into the top of Emma's arm, making her think that perhaps she has hurt herself. Was she too quick to think that she hadn't? Emma's mind swirls into a fog and the blood warms in her veins. She looks up to see who is helping her but her vision blurs into a kaleidoscope of colours. She tries to speak again to the person, to tell them she is okay but her words are lost in the feeling of euphoria washing over her entire body, the words becoming insignificant and pointless. *Let me rest for a moment.*

Emma's mind speaks to itself and she leans back so that she can get comfortable on the lush wet grass below. The water splashing around her is bliss.

Chapter 7

Emma's eyes roll back and a profound look of joy spreads across her face when she settles back onto the grass. *Good*, Bradley thinks, *very good. This is going far better than I could possibly have imagined.*

He immediately scolds himself for getting overconfident. *This isn't the time for congratulating yourself or slapping yourself on the back. Now is the time you need all of your concentration and cunning to get your prize home without anyone noticing.*

Redoubling his concentration, Bradley leaves Emma enjoying her trip on the grass and picks up her bike. He rolls it out of the park and to the back of his car, where he presses the button to release the boot catch.

The bicycle easily fits into the space with the back seats down, and Bradley reaches up to pull the boot closed, he then rushes to open the passenger door so that it is ready to receive Emma.

Before re-entering the park, Bradley takes a second to check the road again. He cannot afford anyone seeing him bring Emma out of the park, and he's relieved to see that all is quiet.

Emma is exactly where he left her, but she seems to have lost conciseness. A horrible thought hits him that he has overdosed her with morphine, but he pushes that thought to the back of his mind. She is still breathing and that's all that matters at the moment.

He has more urgent issues to consider, such as not getting caught.

Bradley struggles to lift Emma off the ground. She is heavy compared to when he lifted Wendy's corpse earlier, and the soggy ground is difficult to contend with. After some slipping and sliding, and no small amount of straining, Bradley manages to lift Emma clear of the ground and cradles her in his arms. He is very cautious with his footing until he reaches the solid ground of the pathway where he quickly moves to the exit. Bradley takes one last look out as best he can with Emma's dead weight in his arms, before stepping out into the open.

No one is around to watch Bradley carry his bundle over to the car or to see him struggle to get it inside. At the last minute, he decides to push the passenger seat all the way back so that he can fit Emma into the footwell of the car, rather than having her on show sitting in his passenger seat. There is also an old blanket in the rear, and he uses it to hide Emma even further by putting it over the top of her.

His prize secured, Bradley quietly shuts the passenger door and then calmly goes around the front of the car to get into the driver's seat.

He doesn't try to turn the car around to go back the way he came; he wants to get clear of the area as quickly as possible, so he drives straight on.

Bradley is absolutely buzzing as he drives away from the park. He can't believe that he actually has Emma in the car with him. He knows that it's not over yet, that there are still hurdles ahead, but he allows himself a small internal celebration when he turns out of the road and onto a new one.

There is one more task to take care of before he can head home to inspect his subject properly. Emma's bike has to be disposed of, and he knows the perfect place to do it. He just happens to be heading in that direction.

Bradley's excitement about getting home could easily cause him to try and race back, but he is careful to check his speed. He'll be home soon enough. The roads are quiet for a Saturday evening, the rain has certainly put people off venturing out, and Bradley quickly reaches the outskirts of the small city. Now, he has a decision to make: into which canal to throw Emma's bike? There are several stretches locally to choose from, and he doesn't want to use one that gets busy with visitors and day-trippers. Bradley decides on the perfect spot that he has come across on his own bike rides previously.

Leaving the main road, the stretch of canal Bradley heads for runs through a farm and is only reachable by taking a dirt track off a country back road. His luck stays with him when he drives off the road and onto the track. No other cars are around to see him make the turn. If there had been, he would have driven past and returned. The last thing he wants is anyone wondering what business a car has driving through a field on a rainy Saturday night.

Parked up near the canal's edge, Bradley pulls the bike out of the car and rolls it over to the water, his headlights showing him the way. At the water's edge, he turns right, rolling the bike off the track and into the field, moving away from the track as far as he dares in the darkness.

This'll do, he thinks, when the light from his headlights fades and he is walking in complete darkness, in the mud.

Emma's bike flies from Bradley's grip and is almost instantly lost in the dark night. Seconds later, a loud splash tells Bradley that another of his tasks is complete and he turns back to his car.

Now, I can head home, he tells himself as he turns the car around, Emma still under her blanket. The car's wheels spin and lose grip on the muddy grass for a moment as he is turning the car, but he manages to get it back onto the track and has soon left the field completely.

Bradley is reversing his car back onto his drive before he knows it.

Reversing on will give him a direct path to carry Emma through the front door. Killing the engine, he glances down at the top of the blanket which doesn't seem to have moved since he placed it there. He worries again about the dosage he gave Emma as he gets out of the car and goes to unlock the front door. His shoes are caked in mud from the field, *a small price to pay*, he thinks as he slips them off on the front step. Stepping inside the house, he puts the muddy shoes down just inside the door to sort out later, and he grabs another pair to put on. Before he goes back out to retrieve his prize, Bradley goes around to open the basement door and turn on the lights. It is going to be difficult enough to somehow carry Emma down the narrow stairs without having to contend with doors and lights.

Taking off his cap and drenched hoodie that would only look out of place if one of his neighbours look out of a window and see him, Bradley's nerves flare as he opens his front door again. Trying to look as casual as possible, as if popping back out to the car to get his phone or something that he's forgotten, Bradley opens the passenger door. The road outside his house is deserted, but before he leans in to pick Emma up, Bradley checks the immediate houses in case any of his neighbours happens to be looking out at the rain.

Curtains are closed, however, and all is quiet. Everyone is in front of their TVs, hiding away from the awful weather, and so Bradley goes for it.

If Bradley thought getting Emma into the car was a struggle, getting her out turns into a nightmare. She is still breathing, to his relief, but her body is a dead weight. Any thought of discreetly leaning in, swiftly picking her up and whizzing her through the front door of the house quickly evaporates. She is wedged into the footwell and Bradley's first attempt to lift her out fails completely. He stands back up, his lungs huffing. He checks the coast is still clear and then goes back in for another attempt. This time, he pulls her by her arms, his foot wedged against the door sill for purchase and Emma starts to rise. Bradley manages to wrestle Emma up far enough to get her backside onto the passenger seat, and then he takes a breather and another look around. He pivots her legs out of the car door, and finally, she is in a position to pick up. Before he goes in for the last lift, he drapes the blanket back over her, covering as much of her as possible, and takes one last scan of the road and neighbouring houses.

Bradley's back and arms take the strain and he forces himself to lift Emma up and out of the car. He won't fail now, no matter how much his muscles protest at the weight. With Emma finally in his arms, Bradley rushes over to the front door, pushing it open with his foot and at last, he carries Emma over the threshold.

There is no way Bradley is going to get Emma into the basement with this lift; she is already starting to slip out of his grasp and his back is threatening to give way. Instead, he kicks the basement door closed and rushes her into the lounge where he drops her onto the settee. Stretching his back out with a sigh of relief, Bradley gets his breath back, standing over Emma for a moment. Leaving Emma where she is, he goes back out to the car, gets his bag out and locks it up before gladly shutting his front door on the sodden rainy night.

Wow, Bradley thinks as the front door bangs shut, *you've done it and nobody saw you, Emma is here.* He feels himself harden at the very thought of Emma's young, fresh body lying on the settee in his lounge. He must get her into her room before he inspects her properly and dresses her for her stay. He won't be able to concentrate on her fully until he does.

A quick look at your new subject won't hurt, *before you try and move her,* he tells himself and goes into the lounge. He leaves her for a second while he meticulously checks that the curtains are fully shut, with no slight gaps for prying eyes.

Then he switches on the lounge light.

Standing over Emma, the blanket still covering her, Bradley's hands tremble.

His fingers take hold of the top of the blanket and he slowly peels it back, his eyes wide in anticipation and wonder.

Bradley isn't disappointed. Emma is more beautiful than he remembered, even in her dishevelled state. Her blonde hair is wet and matted to the sides of her face and any makeup she might have been wearing has been washed away by the rain. She looks so naturally pretty; her flawless fair skin and her full tender pink lips are perfect, and she is so young. At nineteen, she is just starting to blossom, and Bradley is going to be lucky enough to experience her becoming a woman.

Emma's closed eyes and nose fidget as if she is dreaming—or is it the morphine showing her fantastical images on the back of her eyelids? Bradley's uneasiness about her dosage fades, the faint smile on Emma's lips telling him that she is okay and in fact enjoying her trip, which pleases him immensely. He wants her to be happy and as comfortable as possible, even though her treatment will be, at times, difficult and perhaps painful for her.

She will come through the other side, Bradley is confident about that.

She is younger and fitter than his last subject. And once her treatment is complete, she will be content in her new life and Bradley hopes she could even be happy.

Emma's clothes are wet and muddy from her bicycle accident, but Bradley doesn't think she has hurt herself. Thankfully, the settee is leather and will clean up easily, but her bed downstairs is freshly cleaned and made up especially for her.

He is going to have to clean Emma up before she gets into bed.

He decides that he is going to have to strip Emma's muddy clothes off and wash the mud off her, including out of her hair, as there is no other option. Bradley begins with unlacing Emma's running shoes and removing them and the socks from her feet. Her young toes with red painted nails wiggle upon their release, and Bradley realises how much of a struggle this task is going to be. He is already overflowing with desire but must resist any temptation, at least for now, since he wants to get Emma safely into her room as quickly as possible.

Next, Bradley removes Emma's muddy tracksuit bottoms to reveal the strong long legs he has been fantasising over since she approached him outside the coffee shop. They are amazing, and he slowly traces their curves all the way up until his eyes meet the thin white material covering her modestly. Summoning all of his willpower, he forces himself not to linger on the tempting material and he takes off her waterproof jacket.

He has to stop there before he loses all self-control. He has removed the muddy clothing, and the rest will have to wait until she is downstairs.

He takes the muddy clothes out into the kitchen and puts them into a black bag to dispose of. Emma won't need them again. He then gets a large plastic bowl and puts it into the sink. While the bowl fills with hot water, Bradley rushes upstairs to get a sponge, a bottle of shampoo and towels out of the bathroom.

Emma's hair is tricky to clean. It's so long and has a fair amount of mud in it, together with pieces of grass and the odd small leaf. He uses the sponge and has a towel placed under her head to soak up most of the excess water. Her hair done, it doesn't take long for him to wipe her face dry and get the mud off her hands and wrists.

Her clothes have protected the rest of her body from getting muddy.

Satisfied that he has cleaned Emma sufficiently, for now, Bradley pushes the bowl of muddy water to the side to dispose of later, and stands to admire her. He looks down at his prize, who has shown little sign of waking from her morphine-induced coma, even when he sponged her face. She really is magnificent and going to be a joy to work with, he decides. Now, he just needs to get her down the basement stairs.

After some deliberation, Bradley decides to try and get Emma onto his back, piggyback-style, to get her down the narrow stairs. He pulls her up into a sitting position on the settee and then stoops between her legs. Pulling her arms around his neck and holding them tight, Bradley goes to stand. His thighs push him up and Emma rises with him; her legs dangle down behind him but she is up and he carries her towards the basement door.

Only hitting Emma's head and his own a couple of times on the way down, Bradley has managed to get her into the basement. In fact, it is going so well, he takes her straight into her room, turns his back to her bed, and sits them both down onto it.

Emma flops back away from Bradley onto her bed, and with a bit more pushing and pulling, settles into the bed properly.

Bradley even positions a pillow under her head to make her as comfortable as possible.

Excellent. I hope you are happy in your new room, my love. I'll look after you, don't worry, Bradley thinks, as he sits down on the side of the bed next to Emma to get his breath back. He realises that he is worn out after his busy night, mentally as well as physically. He will sleep soundly tonight. *Especially after I and my beautiful new subject have got properly acquainted*, Bradley thinks, as his hand moves to get the hair out of Emma's face and strokes her cheek.

With his excitement threatening to boil over, Bradley stands.

It is time to start Emma's therapy. One of the most important aspects of any treatment is communication, and even subliminal communication can offer great value.

"It is time to get you suitably dressed for bed, my darling Emma. You will need your rest tonight," he tells her. "I have a lovely new nightie for you, and it's my favourite colour red. I hope you like it, as I think you will look amazing in it."

Bradley turns to pick up the nightie he has selected especially for Emma's first night with him. It is sitting on the chair in the corner. Red really is his favourite colour, certainly when it comes to women's nightwear. Bradley unwraps the silky garment, and it feels soft and lush in his hands. He holds it up over Emma's bed as if to show how lucky she is.

"What do you think?" he asks Emma, even though her eyes are closed and she is off in another, drug-fuelled world. He doesn't know if she can hear him, but communication is very important. "The colour will be perfect for you, and you will look so beautiful. Let's get you undressed, shall we, so that you can put it on?" Bradley steps forward.

Chapter 8

The silence of her oblivion is pierced by the sound of a voice, a familiar voice and one that holds no pleasant tones for her.

She knows that as her mind slowly returns from the abyss it has been dwelling in.

Her anger rises, as the disgusting voice won't stop disturbing her rejuvenation that has been taking place while her mind was lost. The sound eats away at her rest, forcing her back to reality, a reality that hangs by the thinnest of threads and has been stretched to its absolute limit.

Air billows into her lungs through her gaping mouth as her back arches and her head goes back. Suddenly, her life has returned to her, and only her confusion of where she is stops her rising and grabbing it immediately with both hands.

Something is covering her face and it wraps around her body. Her newfound strength easily pulls it away, though, and light streams into her grateful eyes.

The weakness she has known for so long has retreated; she feels a power she hasn't known for what could possibly be an eternity.

Standing, her feet feel firm on the ground, the slight dizziness soon dissipating and leaving her head clear. She is totally alert.

"Get away from her, you disgusting, evil pig!" Wendy says firmly to the naked man standing over the young girl in a bed she knows all too well.

Bradley's flabby arse clenches and he freezes in shock, the back of his head afraid to turn to look at his wife, his wife that is surely dead.

"Did you hear me, fucker? Get away from her!"

Wendy's anger and hatred simmer close to boiling point.

Wendy fixes Bradley in a chilling stare, her head tilted forward, as cautiously, he slowly begins to turn to face her. In his hands is a red garment, and Wendy knows exactly what it is. She is dressed in a similar one where she stands.

Below the nightie and the roll of his belly, Bradley's poor excuse for a penis is quickly losing its vigour and reverting from its small erect state to its tiny flaccid one.

Bradley's face is one of shock and disbelief at seeing his wife standing before him.

Thought you'd killed me off, did you? Well, you were wrong, cunt! Wendy's mind screams as the side of her face curls up into a snarl.

"Wendy, my love, I thought I'd lost you," Bradley tells her, regaining some composure. "I'm sorry you had a bad reaction; it wasn't deliberate."

"Not deliberate? You were poisoning me constantly, you sick fuck. And who's that poor girl, your *next* victim?"

"Don't worry about her. She's nothing, not compared to you, but I thought I'd lost you, darling," Bradley pleads.

"Don't darling me."

"Calm down, please Wendy. We can sort this out."

"Have you completely lost your mind, you lunatic? You cut Brian's throat in front of my eyes and imprisoned me in that fucking room for months, feeding me poison. Now you've abducted a young girl, and I'm supposed to calm down? What is wrong with you?"

"Nothing's wrong with me, that you didn't do to me Wendy, now calm down before you regret it," Bradley says, his confidence returning.

Wendy sees the change in Bradley's demeanour as his initial shock of her standing before him subsides, his evil side rising once more.

He obviously wasn't expecting me to wake up again, Wendy thinks, *and now that I am, he probably thinks it's business as usual. Well, he's going to be sorely mistaken.*

"This has gone way too far, Jonathan. I won't let you unleash your perverted lunacy on that girl. I'm leaving and I'm going to take her with me. Now get out of my way," Wendy growls.

"Or what? You aren't going anywhere. You belong here with me," Bradley says, his arms dropping to his sides, the red material dropping to the floor from his hand.

"Get out of my way!" Wendy screams.

Bradley doesn't move an inch. The only thing that does move is his mouth that spreads, to smirk back at Wendy. Wendy takes a step forward and sees Bradley's hands curl into fists, ready to fight, the muscles in his arms tensing. She has felt the force of those fists before, many times, and once just the sight of them had been enough for her to back down. That was then, but they hold no fear for her now.

She now knows pain far worse than Bradley's feeble fists can offer.

"You know you can't beat me, my love. I don't want to have to hit you, but I will. I'll hit you until you're black and blue. So, be reasonable, come back into your room and sit down. Your new roommate will wake soon and I can introduce the two of you. I think the two of you will become close friends," Bradley's mouth spews.

Wendy takes another step forward, her toes gripping the carpet beneath them.

"If I stay, will you let the girl go?" Wendy asks.

"No, that isn't going to happen, but if you're with her, at least you can look after her, can't you?"

"Yes, I suppose I can," Wendy agrees, her rage escalating inside her.

"Good, I'm glad you can see that. Please come and sit down; it'll be better for you this time, I promise."

"Will it really?" Wendy asks, taking another step forward as she sees Bradley's fists relax.

"Honestly, I know where I went wrong and it won't happen again," Bradley says and moves to the side to allow Wendy to pass and return to her room.

Another step forward is taken, and then another, Bradley's smirk turning into a smile of satisfaction and victory. Wendy takes her last step to draw level with Bradley in perfect unison to her anger boiling over. She channels her rage into her right leg, which shoots up with a force that astounds Wendy. The knee hammers into the tiny penis and testicles dangling in Bradley's crotch. A sickening loud crunching sound escapes before Bradley has a chance to draw breath to scream. His body buckles in two as the pain doubles him up, and then a shrill screaming bursts out of his gaping mouth, tears streaming from his eyes.

Wendy's aim is perfect, especially when the size of the target is considered.

Bradley drops to the floor in agony, one well-placed blow having taken him out.

Wendy quickly grabs the padlock off the cage door to throw across the basement. She won't allow him the chance of locking the door if he gets up. Moving past the crying and whining heap on the floor, Wendy goes to get the girl; she will drag her out if she must.

"Wake up," Wendy shouts into the girl's face while shaking her shoulders.

The pretty girl is out of it though and doesn't respond to Wendy's attempts to wake her. Wendy pulls at the girl's arm to drag her off the bed and out of the steel cage.

"Get away from her, bitch," Bradley snarls at Wendy, pulling himself up on the bed to get to his feet.

Wendy stops her attempts to move the girl as she sees Bradley rise.

She didn't think he would recover so quickly from her blow. Back on his feet, Bradley is stooped over, his left hand at his groin, nursing his tender bits. Bradley may be wounded but he is also dangerous, his anger sending blood to his irate face.

"You had your chance, Wendy; you got a lucky blow in, and now you'll pay. I'm gonna tie you to that chair, slit your throat and bury you in the garden, just like I did with your boyfriend," Bradley seethes, his face going a deeper shade of red.

Wendy's muscles tighten at Bradley's vile threatening words.

Fury courses through her body at the memory of Brian's throat spewing out blood.

Wendy bolts at Bradley uncontrollably, dizzy with rage at the pain he has caused her and for what he did to Brian. Her foot rises and plants onto the bed where she springs forward, jumping at the hideous man in front of her.

Bradley's face changes again, from one of evil malice to one of surprise and then panic. Never has he even considered that Wendy would try to take him on directly and fight him.

Wendy is oblivious to any feeling of fear in her as she flies at Bradley.

There is no fear, only rage and hatred. She doesn't mean to fight Bradley; she means to attack and annihilate her cretinous lunatic of a husband.

Bradley's stooped body tries to straighten and move back to defend against Wendy's assault, his hand leaving his bruised tackle to aid his defence. His defence comes too little and too late, as Wendy's element of surprise has Bradley floundering, her attack on him ferocious.

Wendy's weight springs off the bed and she slams into Bradley's chest with an almighty force and he can't stay upright; he stumbles backwards. Only the wall close behind him stops Bradley falling over, but his back whacks into it, knocking the wind out of him.

Wendy falls with Bradley but her feet land under her, and her fall into the wall is broken by Bradley's obese body. Stunned and gasping for breath, Bradley offers no defence to the blows, Wendy's fury raining down into his upper body and face.

Her fists clenched as tight as she can muster, frenzied punches fly into Bradley.

Wendy's anger makes it impossible for her to stop, no matter how bruised and battered her knuckles become, not until she succeeds in putting him down.

Blood starts to pour from Bradley's nose from the repeated hits that Wendy's fists crunch into it, and his legs start to weaken, but he isn't down yet.

His breath returning, his left arm comes up and pushes against Wendy's chest, forcing her to sway backwards and he immediately brings his right arm around.

Bradley's powerful punch crunches horribly into Wendy's jaw, knocking her sideways. And his left hand is ready to swing another punch that smashes into Wendy's right eye.

Wendy is knocked into an excruciating daze by Bradley's two punches, and she feels herself falling backwards. She lands onto the bed behind her and across the legs of the girl lying there.

She blanks out for a moment but almost at once, something unexplainable rips through her, an inhuman raging mania, that feels so powerful and yet so devastatingly terrifying.

Bradley, still dazed himself, feels relief and satisfaction that the two cracking punches he landed have incapacitated Wendy, and the silly bitch is flat out on the bed.

What was she thinking? Time to finish her off. A pity, but this subject is beyond saving, so it'll be more humane to put her out of her misery.

Bradley moves in to deal with Wendy once and for all. He'll make it as quick as possible for his unruly wife. He has never strangled someone before, but he is fascinated by the deed and is interested to watch the life extinguish from Wendy's eyes.

He moves between Wendy's splayed out legs that dangle off the end of the bed.

His excitement builds as he rubs his fingers together, limbering them up to squeeze the life out of his beloved wife.

Blood splatters across Wendy's torso from Bradley's dripping nose as he leans over her between her legs. Surprisingly, considering the recent assault to his groin, Bradley finds that being between Wendy's legs is beginning to arouse him. His arousal brings with it discomfort, however, so he puts his mind to the task at hand and focuses on Wendy's tender neck.

He will check the damage her knee has done to his prized assets when some order has been restored to his basement.

Wendy's eye has swollen badly and is turning black from Bradley's punch.

He was hoping her eyes would be open for her final breath of life.

A deep bruise is also growing on her jaw, Bradley notices as his hands hover above her neck. His wife was a real beauty, he decides as a tinge of regret at her imminent loss makes Bradley hesitate for a moment. *Oh well, it can't be helped*, *you tried your best,* Bradley decides as he brings his opening hands closer in to curl around Wendy's windpipe.

A terrifying burning rage jolts Wendy, snapping her eyes open to save her from spiralling into its unforgiving clutches. The rage retreats from the forefront of her mind, distracted by the silhouette of Bradley hovering above her.

Excellent, Bradley thinks excitedly, as Wendy's eyes open to witness her own death, just as his fingers brush around her soft neck. Her face distorts when he begins to apply pressure, the distortion twisting grotesquely with every ounce of pressure he applies. Wendy's twisted face doesn't satisfy Bradley as he thought it would; it terrifies him, her piercing eyes drilling into his with evil hatred. He increases the pressure to her neck rapidly in panic, now wanting to just get her strangulation over with, as froth bubbles through her clenched teeth.

The pressure around her neck is formidable, and Wendy's lungs are completely cut off from the air, and they starve. Her hatred for Bradley is overpowering though, and she stares into his ugly, demented face until her vision is blocked by the flashing colours of a million stars in her pupils, formed by her brain's lack of oxygen.

Wendy's life is slipping from her grasp, or has it already been extinguished by the cruel hands of her husband squeezing the life out of her?

She doesn't know if she is alive or dead.

She has long since stopped caring, but there is one thing that has to be done before her end is met.

Dropping her resistance, Wendy allows the manic rage to flood in and take hold of her being. Her soul is thrown aside to be replaced by the raging beast that has hungered inside her belly for so long. Incredibly powerful arms push the beast up off the bed, buckling Bradley's arms as it rises. Wendy's gruesome face terrifies Bradley to his core as he flounders to understand the possession that has taken hold of his wife, that he is powerless to hold back.

Her evil eyes burn into his, that are wide and pleading for mercy.

There is no mercy to be given, as the beast is sitting upright and its arms flash through the air to grab onto his, to rip them from around its neck.

Bradley is pulled back down, back onto the bed and onto the beast's waiting, cavernous mouth. Only a whimper escapes Bradley's throat when teeth puncture into the side of his neck, slicing deep into his flesh, severing his veins and arteries. The meat is raw and greedily gobbled down into the beast, Bradley's flowing blood easing its passage.

No bright light is shining to welcome Bradley's sudden demise.

He isn't afforded the slightest glimmer of salvation, only the pitch blackness of a fearful oblivion to welcome him… for now.

Chapter 9

Something moves at Wendy's back. Underneath her, it jabs into her ribcage painfully. Gradually, the memory of the young girl lying on the bed returns, and she knows that it is one of the girl's limbs sticking into her. The rage that took hold of Wendy has been drawn back, but it festers close to the surface, prodding to be released again.

She has to fight to keep it at bay, fearful that if it is allowed to return, it will overwhelm her completely and she will never have the strength to control it again.

A dead weight presses onto her front—Bradley, whose grizzly wound in the side of his neck hovers only inches above Wendy's face. Disgusting blood and pus leak out of the hole and slither down across Wendy's lower neck and shoulder.

A rancid taste sits in Wendy's mouth, infecting her throat and winding down into her gut.

It was no nightmare; it was her own teeth that bit the chunk of flesh from Bradley's neck, and her mouth that swallowed it into her body. She knows that she did it, but it feels as though it was someone or something else that took the bite, just using her mouth as a vessel.

Wendy gags uncontrollably at the thought of the flesh sliding down into her insides. Bradley's body, on top of her, wobbles in time with Wendy's gags, the motion forcing more putrid slime to ooze from his open wound and onto her, making Wendy's gags increase.

She shuts her eyes from the scene for a moment, and brings her gagging under control, until finally, her stomach settles, still intact.

Trapped on the bed under Bradley's weight, claustrophobia begins to close in on Wendy. She has to escape before her panic escalates, and she bends her arms up and onto the body's chest and shoulders.

Pushing with all her might, Wendy manages to shift the body sideways, sliding it across her, the bodily fluid between them beginning to grease its path.

With her eyes tight shut, Wendy feels the body begin to move under its own weight as it slides down off her, until all at once it falls from on top of her. Bradley's body falls off the bed, hitting the floor with a chilling, but satisfying thud.

Free of the weight pressing down, Wendy's lungs gulp down a greedy portion of air and the decent amount of oxygen revitalises Wendy, whose eyes open again and her head pops up off the bed.

Looking around the room that Wendy knows as well as the back of her hand, all is strangely quiet. With her confidence building, her arms push her up further, until she is sitting on the end of the bed. The back of her ribs ache, but the ache is fading quickly now that the girl's foot isn't jammed against them. Sitting there, she tries to understand what has just taken place, but she can't get her head around it. She had bitten into Bradley's neck as if it were a juicy piece of steak, and it tasted just as delicious when it touched her taste buds.

That taste has turned rancid now that she is herself again, and the memory terrifies her; it is so confusing, and embarrassing. Wendy's head looks down to see the torrid remnants of her meal covering her chest, staining her skin dark red as well as the nightdress she is wearing.

On her left, next to her feet, the body of Bradley is rigid where it landed.

Wendy feels no pity for her monstrous husband, of whom she is finally free.

He deserved the terrifying end that his shocked staring eyes convey. She doesn't ponder over his demise. All she feels is relief and she stands up off the bed, turning.

The young girl, the one Bradley was preparing to attack, is still unconscious, her eyes closed but her chest moving. Wendy doesn't think Bradley managed to carry out any of his twisted fantasies that he no doubt planned to inflict on the poor girl. Her top still covers her upper body and her knickers are still covering her intimate parts.

It seems that Wendy awoke from her stupor just in time to save her.

Turning away, Wendy steps over Bradley's legs and begs that her water jug is full, as she goes over to the table it sits on. *Thank God for small mercies*, she thinks as she sees that the large jug is brimming with water. Before she reaches for the water she craves so much, she pulls the straps of her nightie off her shoulders and lets it slip down her body and drop to the floor, kicking it away when it lands. Only then does she reach for the jug, lifting it straight to her lips. The cool water feels amazing in her mouth, but she resists gulping down her first mouthful, instead swilling it around vigorously.

Turning, she spits the mouthful of dregs out and over the corpse on the floor, taking great satisfaction in the act of disrespect when the water splatters over Bradley.

Then she drinks, the gorgeous water sliding down her throat and into her belly, to clean her insides. Her mouth still open, Wendy lifts the jug up and over her face, pouring the water over her skin to let it wash down her chest. Chills shiver up her back as the cold water shocks her skin but she relishes it, savours its cleaning powers. Her only regret is that the jug isn't bigger, that there isn't an endless amount of water to bathe her. She has to force herself to stop pouring when the jug is about half spent, and she puts it back onto the table.

Some of Bradley's scum has been washed off of her skin, she sees, but there is still plenty clinging to her. Wendy takes one of the two small hand towels she was permitted of the handrail mounted on the wall above the table, and she starts to scrub herself off, the towel staining darker with each stroke. Having scrubbed off as much of the scum as possible, until the towel is completely stained with Bradley's putrid blood, Wendy picks up the jug again.

This time, she empties every drop of water from the jug, ensuring that the water is spread as far as possible over her face, chest, and body. Using the second-hand towel to dry herself off as much as she can with the small towel, she feels a relief that at least most of the scum has been washed from her, when she is finished. Discarding the hand towel, which is too deeply stained now, Wendy suddenly feels exposed in her naked state.

Next to the cage's door is a pile of clothes, Bradley's clothes, the ones he recently took off in preparation for his sordid act. *I have just washed that lunatic off me, am I really going to put his clothes on now?* Wendy asks herself.

She has no other option; she wants to get out of this prison as soon as possible, and there is no way she is going to search the house for another set of clothes to get dressed in.

Wendy has endured far worse at Bradley's hands than put on his stinking clothes but she hates every second of the process. In fact, she can only bring herself to put on his t-shirt and joggers; everything else, she leaves in the pile inside the cage.

Her freedom has been hard-fought and Wendy looks to the other end of the basement, towards the stairs that will lead her away from this hellhole.

She cannot complete her escape yet though, no matter how desperate she is to finally leave, to feel the fresh air and the sky above her. Wendy won't feel that though, not without taking the young girl to feel it with her, and so she turns back.

Bradley's torso blocks the narrow gap that leads down the side of the bed.

Wendy stretches her leg over it, trying not to step in anything disgusting on the floor, but inevitably feels gunk squidging between her toes. Ignoring her revulsion, she realises that she has no idea what the girl's name is and so she can't use it to try and rouse her from her unconscious state. Wendy also has no idea what Bradley has done to the girl to knock her out. Did he smash her over the head, or has he drugged her? Knowing Bradley, it could be either, but Wendy guesses that he has drugged her and if she had to guess further, she would guess that it's morphine he used as his drug of choice, as he did with her.

Taking hold of the girl's shoulders, Wendy shakes her forcefully, telling her to 'wake up', but at first, she gets no reaction. The poor girl is obviously heavily sedated. After several attempts, however, the girl's eyes open a tiny amount and she slurs something incomprehensible; it isn't much but the reaction spurs Wendy on.

"It's time to wake up now, you need to get home. Your parents will be worried where you are," Wendy pleads, longing to get out of the house and away from Bradley, even though he is dead.

Little by little, Wendy's persistence starts to work and the girl responds slightly more. Encouraged, Wendy takes hold of both of the girl's hands and pulls her up into a sitting position on the bed, talking to her constantly. A mumble interrupts Wendy's chatter, inaudible, but it is progress, slow progress. *Wake up now,* Wendy's mind pleads.

"What is your name?" Wendy asks, trying to engage with the girl more, trying to get her brain to start working again.

Wendy receives another mumbled response, that sounds like 'Ma," but she could have misheard.

"Say that again? I didn't hear you properly," Wendy encourages.

The girl mumbles, "Emma," and this time, Wendy recognises the word, she thinks.

"Emma, is that right, is your name, Emma?"

The girl jerks her upper body in Wendy's arms, making her head go up and down, and Wendy takes that as confirmation.

"Good, Emma, that's very good; shall we get you up and get you home?"

Again, Emma jerks to agree, and Wendy decides that now is the time to try and get Emma to her feet. She is far from lucid, but maybe with her help, there is a chance of getting Emma out of this godforsaken house.

This isn't going to be easy, Wendy decides as she tries to move back around the bed. She needs to keep Emma in her seated position and hold her arms whilst she steps over Bradley. Wendy ignores the repulsive gunk she is stepping in, and her concentration is on keeping Emma in place so that she can pull her off the end of the bed, the most direct route.

After a considerable amount of effort, Wendy has managed to position Emma so that her legs are dangling over the end of the bed and her feet touching the floor; now to get her upright. "Come on, Emma, it's time to stand up now," Wendy orders and then pulls on Emma's arms to help her to her feet.

Leaning back, Wendy pulls Emma's arms, her moist feet threatening to slip on the floor below. More words of encouragement are issued by Wendy, and gradually, Emma's behind rises from the bed. Then, thankfully, Emma is standing.

"Very good," Wendy encourages as she quickly positions herself under one of Emma's arms to support her. Then, almost miraculously, as Wendy instructs, Emma puts one foot in front of the other and they begin to walk out of the cage and into the basement beyond.

The relief Wendy feels as they squeeze through the open door of the cage is cut short and turns to terror as a loud grunt echoes behind her, from inside the cage.

You must have imagined it. Wendy tries to fool herself, too scared to acknowledge the only other option. Bradley is dead and there is no one else to make that noise. Another grunt sounds, dispelling her first desperate thought and sending fear and loathing coursing through her body. *Bradley must still be alive; you didn't kill him, and he is rising behind you to reap his revenge.* Wendy panics and all but drags Emma to the other side of the basement, every sinew in her body terrified that at any moment, a hand is going to touch her from behind.

The basement stairs are close and inviting but getting up them with Emma is going to take time and she doesn't know if she has any. She sees Bradley's black chair behind his desk and it is pointing in their direction, offering its services. Wendy hauls Emma around and dumps her onto the chair before summoning all of her courage to turn and look back in the direction of the cage.

A slither of relief hits Wendy when she doesn't see Bradley standing, but her fear is paralysing at the sight of his body moving on the floor. *Impossible, how can he still be alive*?

Her mind races; he was dead, and she was almost sure of it… almost.

Wendy's shock at seeing Bradley move again is real, as is her dread at knowing that he is alive. She thought she was rid of him forever. Wendy cautiously steps closer to the cage, her mind unable to contemplate continuing with her own life with that depraved monster haunting her. She should call the police who would surely arrest him, but what then? Prison, there is no guarantee, but even if that happened, with the ridiculously short sentences the courts often hand down, he could be out in a few short years ready to terrorise her again. No, she won't let that happen, she refuses to; she will deal with the cretin now, and for good, she promises herself.

Brave thoughts, Wendy thinks, *but what exactly are you going to do about him?* Bradley's body convulses, making Wendy recoil and then a different noise vibrates out of the cage, obnoxious deep coughing and chilling retching. Wendy is revolted by his noise and is frozen in no man's land between Emma and Bradley, desperately trying to think of a plan. Suddenly the horrible noise stops along with the convulsing. *Is that it,* Wendy asks herself, *is he finally dead?*

Wendy's spine shudders when Bradley's body begins to rise from the floor, his arms shaking from the effort, the top of his head appearing above the bed from its hiding place behind it. Her paralysis stiffens as her terror rises; she could run now and get away, get help and come back for Emma, but what about her promise to herself?

In reflex, conquering her fear, Wendy jumps into action. She moves right and grabs the duvet off the basement floor, and in the same motion, takes it to the cage door and throws it the short distance across to where Bradley is struggling up.

The duvet unfurls to a certain degree on its flight, and lands over Bradley and the bed, covering most of Bradley when it settles. It will throw Bradley into darkness and hopefully confusion, buying Wendy a bit of time. She needs to retrieve the padlock she threw across the basement with aplomb after she had kneed Bradley in the bollocks.

The padlock is in the corner of the basement next to the stairs, and it is quickly in Wendy's hand. She then rushes back to the cage and pulls the door swiftly closed, Bradley still flailing around under the duvet when she snaps the padlock shut. Feeling secure behind the locked metal wired door, Wendy watches as Bradley manages to fight his way from under the duvet. He has got himself into a weird, uncomfortable-looking sitting position and his face looks around his caged room as if he were seeing it for the first time.

How do you like your cage? How does it feel? Wendy asks Bradley in her head. Just as she thinks it, Bradley's head turns to see Wendy standing on the other side of the wire; he focuses on her. *Can he read my thoughts?* she wonders as he gazes at her.

Bradley sits there, staring menacingly at Wendy, his head tilted forward. His eyes are evil and unblinking, his torrid neck wound glistening and oozing putrid fluid.

Wendy is caught in that stare for a moment, her mind reeling at his shocking deathly appearance, his skin drained of any colour. She thought he had died, so is Wendy looking at an apparition, his phantom refusing to let her be, here to haunt her for eternity?

Fuck that, Wendy thinks. If he is back to haunt her, he can do it from inside the beloved room that he prided himself on. All at once, Wendy knows what she must do and she brings the staring contest with the monster to an end. Bradley moves inside the cage, his arms pulling on the bed to try and pull himself up, a chilling and low gurgling screech sounding in Wendy's direction.

She doesn't acknowledge his noise, doesn't allow him to see the shock of fear it sends down her spine; no, she is done with him.

The door is heavier than Wendy had thought.

It seemed to glide so easily into place when she had watched Bradley use it to shut her into her dungeon so many times. Gradually, it moves across, each inch seeming to take more and more effort, and she knows that it isn't the door's weight. It's her flagging strength that is the problem. As the door closes, the beast inside becomes more and more agitated, its screeches constant and ear-piercing.

Nearly there, Wendy tells herself, but she jumps back away from the door as a loud crash rings out against the wired frame. *Bradley*, she thinks, *he is on his feet.*

Forcing herself, Wendy goes back to the door to finish her job, adrenaline bringing back at least some of her strength. The door closes faster as she pulls it with increased vigour, until there is only an arm's length to go, and one more concerted effort.

A shadow moves against the light and something bounces on the bed, on the other side of the wire. Wendy nearly falls backwards in terror as Bradley slams into the wire only inches away from her face, as he tries to escape into the small gap remaining.

The wire keeps the ferocious beast at bay, its fingers curling through the mesh, pulling its hideous face closer and closer until it is pressed against it, hatred burning in its eyes.

The beast snarls ferociously at Wendy, its spittle spraying through the holes of the mesh and hitting Wendy's face. She doesn't feel the spray, the beast's terror is overwhelming. She can't move. She is under the beast's ghastly spell.

Shut the door! her mind screams.

Wendy feels her arms pull, the gap closing a little and then she pulls with all her might—and suddenly, the gap has all but gone. Bradley's bone-chilling screech of protest blasts through the vanishing gap, but one final push shuts the door, cutting off the horrific noise. Bradley is gone.

Wendy drops to her knees, gasping from the effort and the fear. She is spent and starts sobbing uncontrollably. Now, she finds herself on her knees, her head pressed against the door, in the corner of the basement, Wendy cries. She cries for the torture she has been subjected to, she cries for Brian, and she cries from exhaustion. Tears stream down her cheeks and spill down onto her legs and the floor below, and she doesn't know if she will ever stop crying.

Her mind is a jumble, teetering on the edge of falling into madness. She feels so lost and alone, but then something draws her back from the edge, something important: Emma.

Wendy's arms rise and touch the solid closed door in front of her, and then they push her head up. She leans back onto her feet behind her, her hands moving to her face to dry the tears that have all but stopped.

Pushing against the door to steady herself, Wendy slowly stands, her purpose returning.

Getting Emma back onto her feet was difficult, as she had fallen back into a stupor, but that was easy compared to hauling her up the basement stairs. The faint sounds of Bradley's outrage at being trapped in his tomb had become only intermittent by the time they had reached the top, whereas they had been constant as Wendy had fought to get Emma back to her feet. Wendy will give Bradley one thing; he did a good job of soundproofing his beloved room, and she hopes he enjoys it in there.

As the basement door finally opens, Wendy doesn't know whether to expect daylight to fill her eyes or not. Wendy has no idea if it is day or night and much less what the actual time is. She hoped it would be the daytime, but night will do; anything but that basement.

What now? Wendy thinks as she and Emma reach the hallway of Bradley's house. Her exhaustion makes it difficult to think straight, and she leans Emma up against the stairs, holding her up with the aid of a wooden rung that holds up the bannister so that she can think.

All she wants is to go home, have a long, long shower and then get into bed and sleep—sleep for a week if she wants. It won't be that easy, unfortunately, she knows that. Not with Emma. She needs to get Emma home too. She also knows that she should call the police straight away but there is no phone to use. She didn't see Bradley's downstairs and she can't see a landline up here either. The police won't let her sleep, won't let her rest until all of their questions have been answered and the thought of that fills her with dread.

Should I take Emma to the hospital, or should I go myself, Wendy thinks? She definitely should, but again, how? It's all too much to think about. *Just get yourself home and think about it there. The key is under the stone mushroom near the front door; it's not far, and you can get Emma there. Her legs are starting to work.* Wendy's decision is made, and her brain won't process anything more. She just wants to get home; it isn't far, after all...

Chapter 10

"I can't believe we are going to be apart for Christmas. You can still come home with me to my parents. They would love to have you," Lisa says to Matt who is beside her in bed.

"Umm," Matt replies, knowing full well Lisa's parents would not love that at all, especially her dad.

"Why don't you?"

"I can't. My dad's expecting me, isn't he? I've got to catch up on my studies anyway, and if I'm with you, I won't get anything done, will I?" Matt insists.

"Why, do I distract you, lover?" Lisa teases, stroking her foot up Matt's leg.

"I suppose so," Matt teases back, smiling.

"Hey!" Lisa laughs. "Seriously, it will be more fun than spending it with 'Jonathan'."

"That's my dad you're talking about. I know he's a funny one but he's still my dad, and I hardly ever see him. It will be a good opportunity to kill two birds with one stone, especially as mum's away for Christmas anyway. I also want to see Wendy, my stepmum."

"I'm just going to miss you, that's all," Lisa sulks.

"We'll both be back in Durham before we know it," Matt points out.

"But still, it's Christmas."

"I'll just have to give you your present early, then, won't I?" Matt says, laughing and making a move to get on top of Lisa.

"I want more than that for Christmas," Lisa chuckles, spreading her legs for Matt.

Matt wakes up early in a cold sweat, Lisa breathing heavily, still asleep next to him. It's unusual for him to have nightmares and this one has scared him awake; his heart is racing. Thankfully, the sun is starting to come up and the light eases his fright and immediately starts to fade his horrible dream. Already, he is struggling to remember the details, but his dad was involved; he was evil and brandishing a knife, threatening to stab his mum. Wendy was in the dream too, protecting him from his dad and trying to get him to put the knife down. A chill runs down Matt's back at the fleeting, but still disturbing memory.

He turns over to face Lisa, trying to dispel the nightmare further, confused as to why he would dream that about his dad. *Put it out of your mind; it was only a nightmare*, Matt tells himself, *you don't want that hanging over you when you see Dad later.*

Matt can't quite decide whether he is looking forward to seeing his dad or not. They were close when Matt was small but have been drifting apart for years. The drifting began when his mum and dad split up and divorced when Matt was only seven years old. Matt lived with his mum and saw a lot of his dad too, staying at his regularly, but it was inevitable that things between them would change. Wendy came into Matt's life a year or so later, and she was fantastic. She had no children of her own and doted on Matt, meaning his dad took more of a back seat to some extent, when Matt was with them. Matt grew older and became more interested in hanging out with his friends than seeing his dad, although he did still see him. Then, Dad and Wendy moved to Lemsfield, still close to Matt but not as close, and finally, Wendy and his dad split up too. Matt had just started uni when that happened but it affected him. He loved Wendy, and he felt she was a second mother to him. Matt saw the change in his dad over the years after the divorce. Matt remembers that, even though he was young. The biggest change happened when he split from Wendy; however, he became almost a different person, one who sometimes worried Matt.

Be positive, Matt tells himself, *this will be a great chance for you and Dad to spend some time together and bond again.* Matt's mind settles somewhat, and he soon finds himself drifting back off to sleep.

As usual, the rush to reach the train station in time is manic. Matt is up and ready in ample time, his reasonably sized case sitting by the door, gathering dust. But it is panic stations as usual with Lisa. She refuses to get out of bed, even after she has finished the tea Matt has brought her. She then decides she is running late, not that she lets that fact encroach on her standard extended shower time. Matt is sure it only ends when she is having trouble breathing because of the build-up of steam in the bathroom.

After that, she never manages to get out of second gear whilst undertaking her beautification regime, and only then does she decide to pack.

Sometimes, Matt doesn't know whether to laugh or cry at her complete lack of urgency, but it is one thing being late arriving at the pub, and quite another missing his train.

When they eventually arrive at the station, Matt barely has time to give Lisa a kiss and say goodbye before he has to run to catch his train. Lisa doesn't look impressed at not receiving a proper Christmas farewell. She doesn't have to worry, though; her train isn't due for another half an hour after Matt's has departed, and anyway, Durham train station is hardly Casablanca.

His late boarding onto the train leaves Matt with no seating options, much to his dismay. *So much for a nice, chilled journey,* he thinks, standing there, crammed in the aisle, all thoughts of a possible snooze on the way now vanished.

He must remember to thank Lisa for getting them to the station at the last minute.

Eventually, with only half an hour of journey time to go, the train carriage thins out and Matt gratefully helps himself to a window seat. The opportunity to take a nap has passed. It isn't even worth attempting with so little time left before he arrives in Lemsfield. Instead, Matt watches the world fly by outside his window as the sun starts to depart, despite it only being late afternoon. His thoughts are of Lisa, and he wonders what will happen to them after Christmas? They will both be starting their last semester at uni and they have made no plans for their relationship past their time in Durham. Perhaps that will be the best place to leave their relationship and remember the good times, and not try to turn their time together into something it's not? Matt is extremely fond of Lisa. She is beautiful and so much fun, if not a bit hair-brained, but does he love her? He isn't sure about that. Matt has an inkling that she is of the same mind, but if she's not, then why hasn't she pushed to make plans and talk about their future together? He is sure he will be moving back home with his mum, at least in the short term when he rides this train home for the last time, in only a few short months. Lisa lives almost in the opposite direction and Matt isn't interested in trying the long-distance relationship debacle. In the end, Matt decides that it is something they need to discuss and not skirt around like they usually do, if and when the subject arises.

His thoughts turn to his dad and what it's going to be like spending so much time with him over Christmas. Matt has spent no more than a weekend with him in more years than he cares to remember, and that includes when he was still with Wendy. A weekend is easy to fill, but a week or so could get awkward. *Don't be ridiculous* Matt tells himself, *he's your dad.*

Surely you can spend a week with him and not feel awkward? Matt hopes that is true, but his dad's character is becoming alien to him recently and last night's nightmare isn't adding to his confidence.

Matt's train approaches Lemsfield, a city easy to spot. Its towering cathedral spires light up the night, marking it like a pin in a map. The train rolls into the station in the early evening and as it eases to a stop, Matt sees a large clock on the platform—illuminated only by manmade light—confirming the train has arrived on time.

Having disembarked, Matt heads straight for the exit. By now he's as familiar with the station's layout as he is with the small city centre, which he has to walk through to get to his dad's house.

Lemsfield's centre is lit up like a Christmas tree and bustling with throngs of people. Christmas shoppers are out in force and are sure to find that unique gift they are searching for in one of the quirky shops in the main shopping area or hidden away down one of the old narrow alleyways. There is no piped Christmas music, not in this shopping centre. The festive musical backdrop is real, provided by carol singers in the main square, with a brass band waiting in the wings to headline and belt out everyone's favourite Christmas tunes.

The numerous bars and restaurants are doing a roaring trade, jam-packed with people out for their Christmas parties. The Christmas spirit begins to rub off on Matt, and whilst he dreads the shopping part of the festive period, he is more than happy to join in the celebrating with a pint or two. He wonders if he will be able to convince his dad to join in the revelry. What better way to break the ice properly between the two of them again?

Matt finds he has a spring in his step as he walks through the crowds. What this city lacks in size, it certainly makes up for in character and Matt can certainly understand why his dad and Wendy moved to the area.

As he leaves the small centre area, Matt finds himself itching to get back and join in the festivities. Luckily, the walk to his dad's house will be short and Matt plans to drop his bag and drag his dad out of the house for a drink, if he has to, and maybe a bite to eat. It may be the Christmas spirit but he finds himself really looking forward to seeing his dad and hopefully reconnecting with him over the holiday period.

Good, Matt thinks as he approaches the house; his dad's car is on the drive and the lights are on, so he must be home. He fishes his keys out of his pocket, finding the front door key as he walks up the drive next to the car.

Matt gives the door a knock as he turns the key and pushes the door open. It isn't often he lets himself into the house, and although he is expected today, he didn't confirm with his dad what time he would be arriving, so a polite knock seems a good idea.

"Dad," Matt calls out as he steps inside, but he gets no reply. "Dad," he shouts louder, "I'm here?" still nothing.

Strange, Matt thinks as he looks around. A pair of running shoes have been discarded next to the front door. They are caked in dry mud and look like his dad's size. Matt wonders where his dad has been to get them so muddy, since it isn't like him to go anywhere unless it's in his car or on his beloved bike. Only the hall light is on, and the rest of the ground floor is in darkness, as is upstairs by the looks of it. Suddenly, Matt knows where his dad will be and rolls his eyes for not thinking of it immediately.

He pushes his case out of the way of the front door and takes his coat off before he goes to find his dad in his bolthole. The basement light is switched on, confirming Matt's suspicion that his dad must be in his favourite room in the house, and he starts to descend the stairs, calling out 'Dad' as he goes. But again, there is no reply and when he reaches the bottom of the stairs, there is no sign of his dad in the basement. It is empty. In fact, the computer is switched off and there is nothing to suggest his dad has been down here recently. *Perhaps he just forgot to turn off the light?* Matt wonders, although his dad is famous for insisting that all lights are switched off when you leave a room, as most dads do, Matt suspects.

With his confusion mounting, Matt climbs back up the stairs and leaves the basement, turning off the light as he goes. He checks the lounge in case his dad has fallen asleep in the dark waiting for Matt's arrival. Nothing. The kitchen is also empty, so Matt goes to check upstairs, grabbing his case on the way to take up with him. No one is home, Matt decides after dropping his case into the guest bedroom. *Oh well,* Matt thinks, *I'll put the kettle on then give him a ring*. Or he might have a cheeky beer if there are any in the fridge, not that Matt holds out much hope of his dad having beers in the fridge.

Just as Matt feared, the fridge is devoid of beer so he puts the kettle on and then pulls his phone out of his pocket. Frustratingly, his dad's phone goes straight to voicemail, so Matt leaves a short message to let his dad know he's arrived. He then heads outside to check if his dad's bike has gone, but it's still there.

Pouring himself a coffee, Matt is at a loss as to where his dad might be. The only possibility he can think of is that he's popped into town for something, perhaps some last-minute supplies for dinner? Matt really hopes so, because his hunger is building and he doesn't mind if they eat in or out tonight, as long as they have a drink after. Taking his coffee with him, Matt goes into the lounge to watch some TV and wait for his dad to come home. There isn't much else he can do.

After an hour of watching crap on the TV—there are no paid-for TV subscriptions in this house—and trying his dad's phone once again, Matt begins to worry. He cannot think where his dad could be. He knew Matt was arriving today and yet, he seems to have disappeared. There is only one person Matt can think of who might be able to shed some light on where his dad is: Wendy, and he decides to give her a call.

'Bloody hell!" Matt says to himself when her phone also goes straight to voicemail. What is he supposed to do now? He hasn't a clue.

After watching another twenty minutes of torrid television, Matt's hunger has reached a point where it has to be dealt with, which isn't surprising as it's nearly eight o'clock. He uses his phone and orders a couple of pizzas and some sides, hoping his dad will be home in time to share the meal with him.

With his pizza long since eaten and one in the fridge in case his dad does decide to come home, Matt is more than a little worried and more than a little pissed off.

The time is approaching ten-thirty and he has still not been able to get hold of his dad or Wendy. In fact, the only saving grace of the night so far is that a half-decent film came onto the TV, but even that will be coming to an end shortly.

Just as the film ends, Matt's phone lights up and starts to ring. Matt hits mute on the TV, but his relief is short-lived. However, it is Lisa phoning him and not his dad.

"Hey, babe," Lisa says. "Sorry I didn't phone earlier; I've only just got home. My mum picked me up from the station and we went straight to meet my family at the pub to eat."

"And to have a drink?" Matt says jealously, noticing Lisa's words slurring slightly as she talks.

"I might have had one or two," Lisa giggles. "How's your night been?"

"Terrible. My dad wasn't home when I got here, and I can't get hold of him on his phone. I don't know where he is."

"He's not there now?" Lisa asks.

"No, I'm getting a bit worried, to be honest."

"I'm not surprised you're worried. He knew you were arriving today, didn't he? You told him the right day?"

"Of course, I told him the right day," Matt insists, but also suddenly doubts himself.

"I was only checking. What are you going to do?" Lisa asks concerned.

"I don't know. I've thought about phoning the police, I must admit."

"Maybe he just had to go out and his phone died. Why don't you get to bed and see if he's there in the morning?"

"There isn't much else I can do, not that I can think of, anyway," Matt agrees.

"I'm sure there's a simple explanation, Matt. Try not to worry."

"You're probably right, but it's hard not to."

"I know, get some sleep and I'm sure everything will be okay in the morning. You'll probably wake to find your dad home," Lisa reassures.

"I hope you're right, but it's very strange."

"Yes, but you're a big boy and can look after yourself," Lisa teases, giggling.

"How was your night? It sounds like you've had a good time."

"Yes, it was very good. Mum and Dad were there, and my brother and I bumped into some friends from school and had a few Christmas drinks."

"I'd never have guessed," Matt laughs, noticing Lisa's 'couple of drinks' have now moved on to a few. Which in actual fact will mean quite a few.

"Well, it is Christmas after all," Lisa points out.

"Yes, I'm not holding it against you, don't worry," Matt jokes.

"Good," Lisa laughs. "I'm gonna get to bed now, honey. I'm off Christmas shopping in the morning, okay? I'm sure your dad will be home soon; I'll ring you before I go."

"Okay, babe, speak then. Night."

"Goodnight, handsome," Lisa slurs and is then gone.

Matt looks at his phone screen when Lisa hangs up, just in case his dad has tried to phone him while he was talking, and he hasn't noticed.

He hadn't called, so Matt tries his number once more.

But he gets the same voicemail message, and the silence closes in.

Now, he tries to figure out what to do next. Lisa is probably right; his dad will turn up at some point tonight, and so will be here in the morning. Should he go to bed or wait up for his dad to come home? One thing's for sure, Matt has the creeps. Being alone in a pretty unfamiliar house and his dad missing, is making him feel very uneasy.

He isn't yet at the stage of jumping at shadows, but he isn't far off, even nervous to go upstairs, never mind about trying to sleep up there. Getting into bed will only bring cold sweats, the jitters, and plenty of tossing and turning. Matt knows that before he even tries.

He is embarrassed at himself for being such a wuss but tells himself it's understandable, under the circumstances. He decides to bed down on the sofa, with the television on for company. If his dad does arrive home, he can always pretend he fell asleep accidentally. Flicking through the few channels available to find something that can run through the night, he flicks straight past any programmes that might add to his jitters, of which there are a few at this time of night. There is really only one option, the news channel; nothing to scare him on there, he hopes. Matt turns down the volume as much as he dares and leaves the small dim lamp on beside him. He settles back onto the settee, hoping some sleep will come, or that his dad will make an appearance.

Time moves on and Matt's tiredness grows. His eyes are heavy, but the merest noise makes him jump, and his mind goes into overdrive. He knows that the rain and wind outside is the cause of the noise, but that doesn't stop his mind playing tricks on him. His thoughts won't let him settle and they force him to imagine all sorts of frightening scenarios—no matter how much he tries to concentrate his thoughts on other, more pleasant things.

The comfort of the television also begins to lag as he listens to the weather forecast for at least the third time, and then thankfully, when the next weather report plays, Matt has finally drifted off to sleep.

What was that? Matt's mind asks, his heart racing, almost too afraid to open his eyes. Did he dream it, was he asleep, he must have been, he must have dreamt it? Or did the haunting whining sound come from the television, from one of the news reports? Matt tries to settle his nerves, to quench the fear swirling inside him. *It must have been on the television,* he tells himself, as he listens to the quiet voices coming from the TV.

Don't open your eyes. It was just something on the TV. If you open your eyes, you won't be able to go back to sleep. Matt starts to convince himself that the chilling sound was perfectly explainable; he could even have imagined it, and his fears begin to subside. *Stop being a baby. You're a grown man and still afraid of things that go bump in the night, so just go back to sleep.*

The low, deep whining rises again, and this time, Matt cannot fool himself that he dreamt or imagined it. He is conscious, and the ghastly noises are real. Matt pulls his arms closer around himself as he lies on his side on the settee, fear now coursing through his body. His eyes snap open, dreading what they will see as sweat drips across his back.

The living room is empty, bringing a small sigh of relief from Matt as he focuses on the television to see if it might be the source of the awful noise. Two newsreaders are sitting in the studio jabbering between themselves about an unknown, but highly important point.

Tentatively, Matt reaches down to the floor to pick up the TV's remote control. Does he dare mute the volume so that he can hear where the noise is coming from? *You have to,* he tells himself as his finger hovers over the mute button, *you can't cower here all night like a scared rabbit.*

The television's volume cuts off and brings silence to the lounge. Silence, apart from the hideous whining that seems to grow more powerful with the room now in silence. Matt forces himself to sit up so that he can try and place where the noise is coming from.

Lying down isn't going to save you anyway, he tells himself. He moves his head around, trying to get a bearing on where the noise is emanating from. *Is it coming from outside? Perhaps it's a fox or other animal howling at the moon or protesting at the rain?* he asks himself. Before Matt has a chance to decide on the source, or the direction, the whining suddenly stops.

Part of him is relieved it's stopped, but another part is worried that he hasn't solved what had caused the disturbing sound. He's become almost afraid to look around the room in case a spectre's shadow is standing in one of the corners of the room. He dares to move his view, but only to his phone, also on the floor near the base of the settee. The time is only a quarter to two in the morning. It's certainly going to be a very long night if he has to sit on the settee, afraid to look around, never mind move.

Matt struggles to know what to do; he has never been this afraid in his life, and yet he feels stupid for letting a silly noise frighten him so deeply. He wishes he could phone his mum or

Wendy, but his mum is away and Wendy isn't answering. He is sure he could find an excuse to phone either of them.

Minutes pass, and eventually, Matt decides he has to stick with plan A, to lie down again and try and get some sleep. The noise has stopped. *It probably was just an animal outside,* he tells himself and slowly, he lowers himself back down. Fiddling with the remote control, now he can't decide whether to put the volume back on the TV or not, as putting it on only masks the noise and makes him more uncertain.

He decides to leave the volume off, and after an inordinate amount of time, he plucks up the courage to close his eyes again. Matt's eyes are closed but he is wide awake, his heart racing and his brain praying that the animal outside will leave him in peace now.

A muffled bang terrifies Matt and his eyes shoot open again, expecting the worst, but the room is still empty. He is sure that the bang came from inside the house and that it wasn't an animal that made it. A flash of anger hits Matt. *This is getting ridiculous, stop being a wimp and get to the bottom of these noises.*

Matt sits straight up just as another muffled bang vibrates, and this time, the bang is accompanied by the whining noise. The bang came from below, from the basement, and Matt looks down toward the floor. *Of course, it came from the basement,* Matt thinks, *why would it come from anywhere else other than the basement that you thought was empty, for fucks sake?*

Without thinking, Matt stands. He plans to get this settled once and for all, even though every fibre of his body is telling him to curl back up on the settee and wait it out until morning. Matt cautiously walks over to the lounge door, which is ajar, his feet feeling cold and fragile, as though a bone might snap with every step. The sensation in his feet must be because all of his blood has rushed to his heart that pounds like a jackhammer in his chest, but he presses on. Chills run down

Matt's spine, fed by the haunting, whining noise that refuses to cease.

Warily, Matt pulls the lounge door open, his eyes wide, searching for the slightest movement, his body tense, ready to defend itself. The hallway is just as he left it, empty, and he steps out into it; nothing is out of place. He notices that the whining sound is quieter as he leaves the lounge. He's unsure if that's a good or bad sign, especially considering the door to the basement is right next to him now, on his left. Pausing before his hand reaches for its door handle, Matt has a thought and walks past the basement door and goes into the kitchen.

The kitchen knife is alien in his fist as he has never held a knife as a weapon before, but it feels reassuring in his grip, and this time, he does reach for the basement door handle. Gently, he twists the handle, trying to be as quiet as possible. The element of surprise is half the battle; that's what they say, isn't it? The door cracks open just a bit, showing Matt the unwelcoming darkness beyond, but the clear sound of whining he was expecting is missing.

Lifting his right hand towards the light switch mounted on the wall next to the door at the top of the stairs. Matt prepares himself for whatever is making this hideous sound, probably standing in the dark at the top of the stairs. Drawing on all of his courage, the knife gripped tightly, and holding his breath, Matt presses the switch.

Involuntarily, Matt recoils as the light flashes on, his eyes adjusting quickly to the brightness. Nothing is there hiding in the darkness to jump out though, and ever so slowly, Matt opens the basement door. His head edges around the door frame and gradually, the stairs come into view; they too are empty.

Creeping down the stairs, Matt begins to wonder if he is being ridiculous. He's heard a few bumps and funny noises and is acting as if the apocalypse is erupting in his dad's basement. Right now, he would probably take a full-on apocalypse over this spooky haunted house shit.

Just above the bottom of the stairs, Matt stops and listens for any tell-tale noises. He can't see the basement yet, that's around the corner at the bottom of the stairs. He is met with silence, nothing untoward sounding from inside the basement, and he wonders if any noise is still audible back upstairs in the lounge. The silence doesn't quell his fear, however; it intensifies it. Anything could be lurking just around the corner, biding its time, waiting for Matt to step into its lair. His sweaty palm closes tighter around the handle of the knife as he prepares himself to take the plunge forward, into the sinister basement.

Throwing caution to the wind, Matt rushes down the last two steps and turns into the basement in a flash. If anything is lurking, he plans to give them as big a shock as they plan for him. Matt lands in the basement, wielding the knife at head height in one hand, and a fist raised in the other, with his face as angry and fierce as he can muster.

Matt is met by a completely empty basement, just as he left it when he arrived and came down looking for his dad. His head turns, searching for anything that could explain the harrowing noises he could hear back in the lounge. He was sure the banging came from below but there is nothing to explain it, not in the basement. Everything is as it should be.

Lowering the knife, Matt's mind switches from looking for phantoms, to asking himself if he has imagined the whole episode. Perhaps it was a fox outside in the rain, playing a joke on him, or something falling over in the wind. *The fox must be pissing himself at my performance*, Matt thinks, as he turns to go back upstairs, his back feeling exposed nevertheless as he turns.

Chapter 11

Waking with a start, Matt struggles to remember where he is for a moment. His heavy head is overjoyed that sunlight is finally bathing the lounge after his impossibly long and torrid night. He pushes himself up on the settee, hoping it will help clear the dark thoughts still clouding his mind.

Eventually, he must have fallen off to sleep. At what time that was, he couldn't say, but he knows it was past four in the morning. Had the disturbing noises stopped to allow him to sleep or was it just his exhaustion that shut down his brain? The noises continued periodically after he had returned from his escapade in the basement. He didn't know then what was causing them and doesn't know now; all he knows is they scared the shit out of him for most of the night.

Added to that was the constant expectation that his dad would walk in at any moment, that had kept him awake. But his dad *didn't* arrive to relieve him of his fears, and he knows that there is no point going to check his dad's bedroom in case he did. He is missing, and God knows where.

Reaching to pick up his phone off the floor, Matt sees the knife that he's kept close by, just in case. No new messages or missed calls appear, to help Matt solve the mystery of his missing father, so his investigations will have to continue. One thing is for sure; there is no fucking way he is going to spend another night alone in this seemingly haunted house. He will check into a local hotel if he must, and he doesn't care how stupid that might make him look. He won't spend another hour cowering on the settee, either; he'd rather sleep on the street.

He must have got at least three, or four hours sleep, Matt decides as he sees that the time is just past nine-thirty. For a second, he nearly tells himself that it could have been worse, but he quickly corrects himself after deciding that he has never known a night like it. His nerves are still frayed even in the cold light of day, and the knife on the floor still gives him some comfort.

Matt tries to phone his dad and yet again, as expected, there is no answer. Feeling like a lost child, Matt scrolls back through his phone until a number he knows he can rely on is displayed, and within four rings, the phone is answered.

"Hey Matty, I was just thinking about you. How are you getting on with your dad?" His mum's voice instantly calms Matt, even though he knows she is in another country.

"Hi, Mum. I'm really worried. I don't know where he is. He wasn't here when I arrived yesterday evening and he still isn't here; he's been missing all night and his phone just goes straight to voicemail."

"Oh, that's strange; are you sure you told him the right day?"

"Yes, Mum, I'm sure," Matt replies exasperatedly, after Lisa asked him the same question last night.

"Maybe he got his wires crossed and thought you were arriving today?"

"I don't see how. I definitely told him today, and why isn't he answering his phone?" Matt asks.

"I don't know, love. He isn't very good with his phone, as you know. I'm sure there's nothing to worry about, my love. So, you're there by yourself?"

"Yes, all night, and it's really freaked me out. There have been really strange noises going on all night."

"Really, what noises?" his mum asks, concerned, hearing the stress in Matt's voice.

"It started with weird whining sounds and then banging. I thought someone was in the basement but it was empty when I went down to look."

"That doesn't sound very pleasant."

"You can say that again; it scared the crap out of me. What should I do about dad?" Matt asks, praying for his mum to tell him what to do.

"Have you spoken to Wendy?"

"No, she isn't answering either."

"Umm, perhaps they are together, reconciling, and lost track of the day?"

"I don't think so. Dad said he hasn't spoken to her in a while," Matt tells her.

"It's possible though. Have you phoned her today?"

"No, only last night."

"Try her again this morning, and if you can't get her either, you might have to think about going home."

"That'll be a great Christmas. But I'm not staying here again by myself tonight, not again," Matt insists.

"Well you know you can always go home; I'll transfer some money if you need it for a train ticket. Listen, I'm sure your dad will turn up today, but if not, phone me and we'll decide what to do."

"Okay, Mum, thanks. I'll let you know if he turns up," Matt says.

"Please do. I'm sorry I'm not there, but if you have to go home, I'll see if we can get a flight home, okay?"

"No, Mum, there's no need to spoil your holiday. I'll be alright. I'll let you know how I get on."

"Okay, Matty; make sure you phone me because I'll be worried. I love you. Speak in a bit."

"Love you, Mum, speak later." Matt hangs up.

Going home is probably the only option he has if his dad doesn't turn up. His mum is right about that, but he doesn't want to do that unless he absolutely must. Matt scrolls through his phone again until he reaches Wendy's number. *Answer this time, Wendy*, Matt begs as he presses the call button.

Matt's heart skips a beat when a groggy voice says, "Hello."

"Wendy, is that you, it's Matt?"

"Matt," the voice replies, and for a moment, Matt thinks he has rung the wrong number. "How are you? Yes, it's Wendy. Sorry… I've been a bit under the weather."

"You don't sound very well, Wendy, what's the matter?"

"Erm… Oh, I've only just woken and I'm just getting over a bad cold which has knocked me about, but I'm much better now and it's nothing to worry yourself about, Matt." Wendy lies to Matt, not knowing what else to tell him. She cannot bring herself to tell him the truth. "Anyway, how are you? We haven't spoken for far too long!"

"I know, I did try and phone you a few weeks ago, but you must have been busy. Sorry, I didn't try again, you know how it is, busy with uni and things."

"Don't blame yourself, Matt; I haven't been very good with my phone lately, either. How is uni going?" Wendy asks.

"It's okay. I won't be there for much longer now, and I've finished for Christmas already. Do you know where my dad is, by any chance?"

"No, why?" Wendy asks nervously, not wanting to know why Matt is asking.

"I'm spending Christmas with him. Mum's gone away, but he's not here and he's not answering his phone, so I'm getting a bit worried."

"You're at his house now?" Wendy says, shocked.

"Yes, I arrived yesterday but he wasn't here, and he still hasn't returned this morning," Matt replies, wondering why Wendy sounds so surprised.

"Oh Matt, I'm sorry," Wendy tells him, her voice upset.

"What are you sorry for?" Matt asks, both confused and concerned at her reply.

"I think we had better talk properly, Matt. Can you come over to my house?"

"Yes, of course, I want to see you anyway, but you're beginning to worry me, Wendy. What's wrong?"

"I'll tell you everything when you're here, Matt, okay? Can you come at midday, to give me a chance to get ready?"

"Yes, okay. I'll come over then."

"Thank you, Matt. See you in a while."

A long exasperated huff escapes Matt; he has no idea what is going on with his dad, but it certainly sounds as though Wendy can shed some light on it. She didn't sound like her normally bright and bubbly self at all. It must have been a bad cold she caught.

His visit is turning into a nightmare, literally and the sooner he visits Wendy the better; he is now relying on getting at least some answers from her.

Matt sees that the time is already just past ten. By the time he has eaten some breakfast, had a shower and got ready, it won't be far off time to walk over to Wendy's, and the sooner the better.

***

Wendy is in tears when she puts the phone down, as her biggest fear is coming to pass. Poor Matt, the closest thing she will ever have to a child of her own, is going to be devastated when he hears the horrible truth about his father, and she will have no choice but to tell him.

She doesn't know what she hoped would happen with Jonathan after she left that house with Emma. She hasn't been able to deal with it. Only poor Matt has been on her mind and she knew the day would come when they would both have to deal with the truth. She just wished it wasn't so soon. The least she had wanted was to be back to full strength so that she could be there for him fully, to help him through his inevitable trauma.

Wendy pulls her duvet back. Perhaps if the nightmares would stop and she could get a good night's sleep, she would feel more like herself, but Jonathan won't stop haunting her slumber. Nevertheless, she must make herself presentable for Matt; he is going to be in for a big enough shock without seeing her like death warmed up.

Getting out of bed, Wendy can feel her strength returning, although it is a gradual process. How she had managed to drag Emma from the house on that stormy night nearly two weeks ago is still a mystery to her; she had been so weak when she stepped out of the front door. The elation she was anticipating at feeling the fresh air in her lungs hadn't materialised, and all of her concentration was taken up with not collapsing under the effort.

She had managed to drag Emma as far as the park before she had eventually collapsed and blacked out. Her next memory was of a kind voice speaking to her soothingly, and then opening her eyes to be greeted by a nurse, which she would later find out, was two days afterwards.

The medical staff at the hospital had been amazing, and that was only matched by the staff's amazement at Wendy's survival against the odds. One doctor had even mentioned that her blood was so toxic, she had no right to still be breathing and that the blood transfusion she had received had probably saved her life.

She had been closely monitored for the entire duration of her hospital stay, but they were still unsure what the long-term effects on her internal organs would be. She would require continual check-ups. The same doctor had made her promise to attend these check-ups before he agreed to discharge her, two days ago.

Wendy remembers how grateful she was to all of the medical staff as she crosses the landing to take a shower. She also remembers how lucky she is to be able to even take a shower at her leisure once more.

Matt will be here before she knows it, and she is so looking forward to seeing him but dreading it too. Things are going to escalate quickly once she has spoken to him, and that can't be avoided now. She knows it is time to put this terrible part of her life to rest.

Matt isn't the only one entitled to some answers. So is Emma. The poor girl is desperate for them, as are her parents and the police.

Wendy just can't face up to the truth, and her pretence at amnesia has shielded her from it. How could she explain what has happened to her, telling strangers how degraded she had become under Jonathan's hand? Her embarrassment at herself is too much to bear, but to share that embarrassment with others was unthinkable at the time.

Wendy's shield is about to drop. She cannot lie to Matt. He deserves to know the truth, no matter how painful it will be for him to hear. And Emma, a lovely girl, who visited Wendy every day while she was in the hospital… her concern for Wendy's wellbeing was totally genuine.

It is past time that the two talked properly, and when they meet for a coffee in town later, they will, Wendy decides.

There is one major issue that Wendy has with coming clean about Jonathan Bradley, and her appalling ordeal in his basement. Perhaps it is the real reason she has gone to such lengths to hide the whole episode, because it is inexplicable, and terrifies Wendy to her very core.

Wendy counts her blessings as she sits in her favourite chair in the lounge and takes the first sip of her tea. These small luxuries and freedoms were once taken for granted by her, but are no longer. She savours each and every one as she waits for Matt to arrive, pondering her story.

A figure crosses Wendy's view outside the front window, and her apprehension of seeing Matt becomes stifling, her nerves on edge. She has never felt this way about seeing her stepson before. They are so close and it has always been a joy to see him. Wendy doesn't blame herself for what happened and prays that Matt won't either, just as she prays it won't turn him against her.

The figure comes up the drive and Wendy waits with bated breath for Matt to come in. The front door doesn't open, however. Instead, there is a timid knock on the door's glass pane, and confused, Wendy gets up to answer it.

“Matt, come in. Why didn’t you use your key?” Wendy asks, as she sees Matt standing on her front step.

“I didn’t know if I should?” Matt replies, sheepishly.

“Matt, this is your house and it always will be while I’m here. You can come and go as you like; you know that, my love.”

“I know, I’m sorry. I guess I’m just a bit confused, what with Dad missing and with you having something to tell me. I hope he hasn’t done anything to you. I know he hasn’t been himself since the split,” Matt says, stepping inside.

Wendy smiles at Matt, slightly relieved to hear Matt acknowledge his dad’s problems. It won’t make her story any easier for him, but perhaps he will understand what she has done, and maybe he can forgive her.

“Come here and give me a hug. Whatever happens between me and your dad doesn’t change the way I feel about you,” Wendy says, opening her arms to Matt.

Wendy and Matt hug for a moment, enjoying each other’s embrace. Wendy has a tear in her eye as they part, which of course she cannot hide from Matt.

“What’s wrong, Wendy, what’s going on?” Matt asks, concerned for both his dad and for Wendy.

“Come, let’s go and sit in the lounge and I’ll tell you everything. Do you want a drink before we sit?”

“No thanks. I think I just want to know what’s happened,” Matt says as he follows Wendy through to the lounge.

Wendy doesn’t sit back in her favourite chair. She takes a seat on the couch next to it and pads the empty space next to her with her hand, indicating for Matt to sit next to her.

“Matt, I’m going to tell you everything and it’s going to be very difficult for me to say, and for you to hear. I know that you love your dad, but please know that everything I tell you will be the truth. I wouldn't lie to you, Matt. You do know that, don't you?"

"Yes, of course, I know that. I love my dad, but I love you too, Wendy and you're worrying me. Please tell me what's going on," Matt says anxiously.

Wendy looks down at the floor, unable to look Matt in the eye when she begins to tell him what his father has done, and not just what he has done to her, either.

Wendy's story starts even before that fateful night when Jonathan slit Brian's throat. She tells Matt how her relationship with his father has soured and how their subsequent split made his father more and more unstable. Matt understands the early part of Wendy's tale; he even sympathises with her, putting his hand on hers and telling her that he has seen the change in his dad too.

Wendy feels the bond that she has had with Matt since he was a little boy return and strengthen as he consoles her for his dad's behaviour. She raises her head, and her sodden eyes manage to look her stepson in the eye when she begins the sordid part of her story, and the slaughter of Brian.

Matt's hand trembles, holding Wendy's as his face of upset rapidly switches to one of absolute shock and horror, the blood draining from him. Wendy moves on from Brian's murder, telling Matt of the basement, and the months of horrific torture she was subjected to below the house in her dungeon. The meals laced with untold chemicals and poisons she was fed, and the humiliation his father inflicted upon her.

Tears flow down Matt's cheeks as he sits in silence, trying to process Wendy's disturbing, heart-wrenching words, his hand now dripping in sweat as it still trembles in hers. To his credit, Matt doesn't retract his hand to pull away from Wendy, and she loves him for it.

Nearing the end of her horrific story, Wendy tells of how she woke from her stupor to find Jonathan looming over another woman, Emma. Her words stumble, though, and she doesn't know how to continue, to tell Matt of his father's death.

Matt suddenly moves, before Wendy can find the words. He slides closer to Wendy and embraces her, holding her tightly as if to try and protect her from the horror that is still to be told. *Does he know what's coming?* Wendy thinks. *Does he realise that there can be only one ending because of the fact I'm sitting here?*

Wendy doesn't have the answer to that question, but she feels the warmth and strength that Matt is transferring to her, and it gives her the courage to continue.

"I haven't finished yet, Matt," Wendy says, pulling slightly away from him so that she can see him, but not moving too far from his aura.

"I know you haven't, Wendy. I'm so sorry that my dad did this to you, and I know that you're going to tell me you killed him. He is dead, isn't he?" Matt says, without an ounce of malice in his voice, only sadness.

"I hope I did, but I'm not sure it's that straightforward, Matt, unfortunately."

"What do you mean?" Matt says, confused.

"When I woke up and saw Emma, that girl in danger, I couldn't leave her and something inside me rose up."

"What do you mean, rose up?"

"The only way I can think to describe it is pure manic rage, which terrifies me still when I remember its power. The rage took over me, like an out-of-body experience, and I attacked your dad."

"Did he fight back?"

"Yes, to start with, he battered me, and my jaw still aches and my makeup is covering the remnants of the black eye he gave me, but the eyeball is still bloodshot in the corner. Can you see?"

"Yes, I saw it as soon as I came in. I'm so sorry, Wendy," Matt says, looking down, ashamed.

"You have nothing to be sorry about, Matt; this isn't your fault. Your dad became insane, and none of us could have seen it coming. Do you understand?" Wendy insists.

"Yes," Matt says, his head raising a small amount. "What happened then?"

"He tried to strangle me. The bruises on my neck have all but gone, but they are still there faintly," Wendy says, putting her head back to show Matt. "That's when the rage overwhelmed me completely. I felt so strong, Matt, and not even your dad could stop me. I grabbed him and..."

"And what Wendy?"

"And I... I bit into his neck, Matt. I bit so deeply that the blood poured out of his neck and I thought he'd collapsed to die," Wendy says, ashamed of herself, and far too ashamed to tell Matt that she ate the flesh that came away in her teeth.

"Oh my God, that's terrible... I don't mean what you did was terrible, Wendy; you had to do what you had to. I mean, the whole thing was terrible. You said you thought he would die, but didn't he die after that?"

"He was collapsed on the floor not moving, but when I went to shut the room, he got up and tried to attack me again. He looked so evil when he got up, as if the rage had taken him."

"Did you phone the police?" Matt asks.

"I dragged Emma out of the house but then I collapsed in the park. I didn't wake up until two days later in the hospital, and even then, I was very weak. I couldn't face the police and the questions they would have, I'm sorry, Matt. I assumed that he would be dead by then anyway."

Matt's face changes, his eyes distant, and Wendy becomes afraid that he is beginning to have a change of heart and is going to blame her. She almost releases his hand in case he becomes angry, but he suddenly grips it tightly.

"Fucking hell," Matt announces and looks Wendy straight in the eye. "I think he is still alive down there!"

"What! Why do you say that, Matt? Don't joke, it was almost two weeks ago."

"I'm not joking, Wendy," Matt says, and goes on to tell her about his torrid night and his terrifying visit to the basement.

Now, it is Wendy's turn to grip Matt's hand tightly when he goes to pull it away, to stand. Wendy manages to catch him and he stays sitting next to her, a look of bewilderment on his face.

"What are you thinking, Matt?" Wendy asks urgently.

"I'm going to have to go and see, aren't I. How do you open this secret room?"

"No Matt, that's not a good idea. I know he's your dad, but no."

"I have to do something, I can't just leave him in there, alive or dead. If he's alive, he will be going to prison, and if he's dead, he will be buried."

"No Matt," Wendy insists again. "It's too dangerous. You don't know what he's like, especially now. Let's phone the police and let them deal with it."

"I need to go and see if he's alive. He won't hurt me," Matt says, starting to panic.

"Please, Matt, he's not himself. We can phone the police together now, and they will take you around to check. Do it for me, Matt," Wendy says, squeezing Matt's hand.

Matt looks at Wendy in a state of shock for a moment; she doesn't know what he is going to do, and his head must be scrambled.

"Okay, let's phone the police," Matt finally agrees.

Chapter 12

Wendy struggles to keep Matt calm, so that he doesn't bolt off back to his dad's house while they wait for the police, who are taking an eternity to arrive.

It was Wendy who phoned the police. She tried to speak to the detective who had questioned her a few times while she was in the hospital, and who has also visited her at the house since she was discharged.

Detective Inspector Armstrong is a very insistent and well-trodden detective, who Wendy suspects knows full well that she hasn't been telling him everything from the outset. That was her prerogative, but things have changed and she would prefer to speak to him rather than some snotty uniform just out of the academy.

There are awkward long silences while they wait for the police to arrive. Wendy tries to chat to Matt, but his mind is understandably elsewhere. It is something of a relief when Matt volunteers to go into the kitchen to make a cup of tea for them both.

He quickly returns with two steaming mugs, though, but he at least takes a seat to drink his tea instead of pacing the floor in front of the window.

By the time there's a knock at the door, it is past mid-afternoon and the light outside has gone dull. Wendy might have considered switching on her Christmas tree lights if she had found the inclination to put one up this year.

Matt impatiently goes to answer the door, and Wendy hears the familiar voice of Detective Inspector Armstrong out in her hallway, asking Matt who he is, and what his relationship to Mrs Bradley is, but nothing more probing than that, for now.

"Mrs Bradley, very good to see you again. I was pleased to hear you wanted to speak to me," Detective Armstrong says as he enters the lounge, still jotting Matt's details into his small police issue notepad.

"Wendy, please, Detective," Wendy tells the tall middle-aged detective who commands the room in his practical, long dark brown raincoat, for the umpteenth time.

"So, this strapping young man is your stepson, Mrs Bradley?" Armstrong asks, checking the notes from which, only seconds before, he has lifted his pen from.

"That is correct, Detective," Wendy confirms as she watches Matt and Detective Armstrong's partner, a stern-looking woman who has never given her name, enters the lounge.

"And..." Armstrong begins.

"Please take a seat, Detective and I will tell you everything. Would you like a drink before we start?" Wendy cuts him off.

"As you wish, Mrs Bradley, and yes, a cup of coffee for me please. Black, no sugar."

"Would you mind, Matt?" Wendy asks.

Matt takes the detective's partner's order and asks Wendy if she wants a drink, which she does. He heads off to the kitchen, Wendy telling him to also put some biscuits on a plate.

Without waiting for Matt to return, Wendy begins to tell the two police officers the same story she has just revealed to Matt. Armstrong has placed a recording device on the arm of

Wendy's chair after asking her for permission, but his notepad is still close to hand to jot specific details in, any that he deems important.

He soon has his coffee in hand and is listening intently to Wendy's revelations as he raises a biscuit to his mouth with his other hand.

Revealing her story to Matt was traumatic and upsetting, and not only because it was the first time she had told anyone of her ordeal, but also because she knew how devastating it would be for Matt to hear. Matt sits quietly on the other side of the room listening again as Wendy speaks, ready to intervene if Wendy needs his support.

Wendy manages to keep her emotions in check as she tells Detective Armstrong what has happened to her. She actually finds the process cathartic and feels a weight being lifted off her as she finally tells the police of the crimes committed against her by her estranged husband.

Armstrong's gaze is fixed upon Wendy when she starts her statement, utilising his unique and well-practised skill of reading people to ensure his witness is telling him the truth. He processes every word as Wendy's story is revealed, and as she continues, his years of professionalism are overwhelmed by shock and horror.

His guard, that every police officer develops to protect themselves against disturbing events, crumbles. He becomes a normal human being, listening to a distressing and horrific story.

Silence falls over the room when Wendy's statement thankfully comes to an end. Armstrong's face is one of shock and concern, as is his hard-nosed partner's. She is sitting next to him, her pen hovering in mid-air, her notepad forgotten.

Matt gets up and crosses the room to sit on the arm of Wendy's chair, his arm going around her shoulder. "Well done," he tells her. She looks up to him, forcing a smile, her face flushed and her eyes red.

"Thank you for telling us your story, Wendy," Armstrong says, "I'm sorry this awful thing happened to you, and I can't imagine what you have been through."

"Thank you, Detective. I'm afraid that the story doesn't end there, does it, Matt?" Wendy says, taking hold of Matt's hand.

"Matt, have you something to add?" Armstrong says, encouraging Matt to speak.

"I think my father is still alive…"

Detective Armstrong pushes himself up and out of his chair wearily—as if he weights the world on his shoulders—when he has heard Matt's account of his disturbing night at his father's house. He certainly agrees with Matt and Wendy that the noises Matt heard need further investigation.

"Are you willing to attend your father's house with us now, Matt?" Armstrong asks, looking at Matt.

"I am, I want to know what has happened to him, despite what he has done, Detective."

"That is completely understandable, young man," Armstrong agrees. "We also need to speak to Emma as soon as possible," he adds.

"Detective," Wendy says.

"Yes, Mrs Bradley."

"Would you allow me to speak to Emma first? I have arranged to meet her for a coffee in town in about half an hour. I think I owe it to her to tell her what I know happened, at least."

Armstrong glances over to his partner to see what she thinks. She shrugs her shoulders whilst pulling a face to indicate she doesn't mind.

"I think we can allow that, Mrs Bradley, but we would like to meet you there once you have spoken to her. Is that acceptable?" Armstrong offers.

"Quite acceptable, thank you, Detective. You can drop me off in town if you don't mind? I'm not sure I'm up to walking that far yet."

"Okay," Armstrong agrees and then looks at Matt, "Are you ready, Matt?"

"As I'll ever be," Matt replies nervously.

Wendy rides in the back with Matt in the unmarked police car, on the short journey to drop her off in the centre of Lemsfield, where the coffee shop is located. Matt is silent as he contemplates what they might discover at his dad's house and Wendy takes his hand in reassurance.

"Be careful in there, Matt, and let the police do their job. Promise me," Wendy says worriedly.

"I will," Matt says, looking over to her. "I will let you know what we find straight away, okay?"

"Yes, please do. My phone will be on. I'm going to be worried about you until I hear."

"I'm nervous, I must admit," Matt says, stating the obvious. "I'll meet you later at the coffee shop. I would like to meet Emma. Is that okay?"

"Of course, it is."

"And I was wondering if I can stay at yours tonight? I don't want to stay in that place," Matt asks sheepishly.

"Oh Matt, I would love for you to stay with me, you don't have to ask, silly," Wendy beams.

"Thanks," Matt says as the police car pulls up at the side of the road, just outside the shopping centre.

“Will you be okay walking from here, Mrs Bradley?” Armstrong asks from the passenger seat up front.

“Yes, Detective, this will be fine,” Wendy replies, getting herself ready.

“And you will wait for us to meet you and Emma when we’re finished?” Armstrong asks.

“As I said, Detective. Now, please remember you are the police officers, Matt is only there to let you in and show you where to go.”

“Understood, Mrs Bradley. Don’t worry, we know what we’re doing. We will look after him,” Detective Armstrong replies, knowing he has his orders.

Wendy leans over to give Matt a hug and she kisses him on the cheek, telling him to be careful once more before she climbs out of the car. She leans down to tell them all, *good luck,* before she shuts the car door and joins the steady stream of people walking towards the busy shopping centre.

“That’s one tough woman,” Armstrong announces as his partner turns the wheel to drive off.

“She is amazing,” Matt adds from the back seat.

All too soon, the police car is parking up again, across the drive of his dad’s house. Matt eyes the front door with trepidation, the descending darkness adding to the ominous feeling growing inside Matt. He is physically scared to go back inside of the loathsome place, his eyes wandering down to the bottom of the house, where the basement is buried. Is his dad really trapped down there, turned into some kind of horrific creature, a zombie ready to attack? It seems too farfetched to believe, but there is definitely something in that basement.

“Leave the lights off. We don’t want Joe Public congregating, looking for a selfie opportunity,” Armstrong says.

Matt assumes Armstrong is referring to the hidden flashing blue lights with which the police car is probably equipped. He then listens as Armstrong jabbers into his police radio, updating his colleagues of his current situation.

"Right, Matt, let's get moving," Armstrong says, opening his door to get out of the car, as does Matt. "When we're inside, show us where to go, but stay behind us, okay? Let us do our job," Armstrong adds as he comes around the car.

"Yes, Detective," Matt agrees, pulling his keys out of his pocket to open the front door.

Managing to control his trembling hand, Matt pushes his key into the door's lock and turns it, pushing at the same time. Inside, the house is just as Matt left it, there are no unexplained noises to greet them, or anything else untoward.

The two police officers look around cautiously, checking out both the kitchen and the lounge. Matt is relieved that he has picked up the knife from the lounge floor and put it away as the police officers emerge from within there. He suddenly has a horrible thought that the knife he was wielding last night could be the same one used to cut Brian's throat, and a chill runs down his spine.

"Are you okay?" Armstrong asks, hovering outside the closed basement door.

"Yes, it's all just a bit nerve-racking," Matt says, not mentioning the knife, but feeling his face flush as if he is guilty of something.

"It's quite normal to feel that way," Armstrong reassures.

"None of this is normal, not for me at least," Matt points out.

"No, this isn't normal, not for us either."

"Not for anyone, I shouldn't think," Matt adds.

"This is the door to the basement, then?" Armstrong asks, eyeing the door and changing the subject.

“Yes, that’s it,” Matt confirms.

“Okay. Fleck, go and check there aren’t any surprises upstairs,” Armstrong orders his partner.

“Yes, Boss,” she replies and immediately leaves to do just that.

Armstrong stands in front of the door as if guarding it, while Fleck runs up the stairs, his ears pricked, listening out for his partner. It takes Fleck no time at all to check the upper floor, and she is soon coming down the stairs, ready for the main event, nodding at Armstrong as she joins him again.

“Right, Matt, you stay up here while we go down and check out what the situation is,” Armstrong orders Matt, who nods in agreement.

“That’s the light switch,” Matt says, pointing.

Armstrong flicks the switch, and then his hand goes down to the door handle. Matt is almost impressed by his confidence, considering what he has been told is possibly lurking below, but his hand waivers on the door handle for just a second before he pushes the handle.

As it was last night—when Matt forced himself, against his better judgement to open the basement door—nothing is waiting at the top of the stairs. Armstrong leans around the doorframe to give himself a better view down into the basement, but as Matt knows, he only sees down the flight of stairs. The basement itself is out of view.

“This is the police,” Armstrong announces forcefully and professionally. “If there is anybody down there, make yourselves known.”

He pulls his head back, looking at Fleck for a moment, waiting for a reply that doesn’t materialise.

“After you, Boss,” Fleck volunteers.

“Ladies first?” Armstrong offers.

"Thanks, but I don't mind. Age before beauty."

Armstrong rolls his eyes and smiles, which turns into a grimace as his body moves to enter the basement. Matt watches as Armstrong disappears through the door, but Fleck has his back, following him straight in. Matt is both relieved that he isn't the one going down to investigate, but also impatient to know what has happened to his dad, one way or the other.

"It's empty. If there's a door, I can't see it." Matt hears Fleck's voice echo up the stairs.

After a moment's consideration, and with a rush of blood to his head, Matt finds himself descending the stairs into the basement to see what's going on.

He turns into the basement's room to find Armstrong, with his hands on his hips, and Fleck with their backs to him, inspecting the far wall.

"Have you found anything?" Matt asks.

Armstrong's head whips around to look at Matt. "I thought I'd told you to wait upstairs?"

"I just want to see what's going on. I'm worried about my dad."

"Okay, but just stay back until we know what's going on," Armstrong says, his head turning back to the wall.

"There's a hole or something in the corner." Fleck points over to the left.

Armstrong steps nearer to get a closer look, his back bending to lower his head, his hands still perched on his hips. "There's something here," he says, as his hand touches the dark patch in the corner. Armstrong's fingers sink into the wall and something clicks. He quickly glances back at Fleck before his back straightens and his arms pull at the wall.

Amazingly, appearing like an illusion, the wall moves a little as Armstrong pulls, and a quiet whoosh of air confirms what Wendy has told them, that the back wall is, in fact, a folding door.

"Bloody hell," Armstrong utters, coughing and stepping back from the door just as it starts to open, his arm moving across his face until his nose is buried into his sleeve.

Matt wonders what Armstrong is protesting about for a second, until the foul stench hits him. Almost gagging, Matt's arm rises in reflex to smother his own airways, bewildered at what could cause such a putrid stink.

"Something's dead in there then," Fleck reveals, seemingly unfazed and answering Matt's question for him.

"Thank you, Inspector Fleck. I was wondering what it was," Armstrong says sarcastically from behind his arm.

Matt's stomach sinks when Fleck confirms what the smell is, the image of his dad flashing before his eyes. Armstrong must see the concern in Matt's eyes, and quickly gathers himself, his arm lowering from his face as his nostrils get over their initial shock.

"I'm sorry, Matt, it's not looking good. Why don't you wait upstairs while we have a look?" Armstrong offers.

"Thanks, Detective, but I think I'll stay," Matt replies with little conviction.

"As you wish, but I must insist that you stay back while Fleck and I investigate. This is probably going to be a crime scene and we can't allow it to become contaminated any more than it has to be."

"I will," Matt agrees, stepping back a pace.

Taking a deep breath through his nose, to become more accustomed to the stench, Armstrong turns back and reaches for the edge of the door again. The door slides fairly easily and its centre moves outwards as Armstrong pulls.

"There's a cage behind, just as Mrs Bradley told us," Armstrong says as he stops pulling, the door opened only a couple of feet. He then reaches into his raincoat, pulls out a small torch that he swiftly switches on. Square wire sections reflect the torch's light as Armstrong brings the torch around to bear on the pitch-black gap between the wall and the door's edge. Holding the torch above his head, Armstrong moves closer to the exposed wire, his heart racing to see what is beyond the square sections.

Matt is on tenterhooks as he watches Armstrong peer into the darkness, knowing that something was alive in there last night. It must have been, to make those noises. He resists stepping closer to try and catch a view, letting the officers do their job, even though his virgin nose is quickly becoming accustomed to the stench of death.

"There's a bed right next to the wire, with a bedside lamp next to it," Armstrong says after what seems like an age. The beam of light moves right in Armstrong's hand, but it and Armstrong's head come to a sudden stop. "We have a body," he announces, "it is curled up on the floor at the end of the bed."

Matt steps forward, unable to stop himself, his emotions getting the better of him on hearing Armstrong's words.

"Stay back," Fleck orders him sternly, bringing Matt to a frustrating stop.

"Okay, there is one body, I'm afraid. Let's get the door open and see if there is a sign of life," Armstrong says, bringing his torch down so that he can pull the door open fully.

Once the door is moving, it glides smoothly across, folding out and onto itself as it goes until it comes to a stop, flush against the opposite wall. Matt's emotions spiral as the cage beyond is revealed, the bleak scene looking unreal, as if he is watching it on television.

The light from the basement proper, dimly illuminates the space inside the cage, revealing the grim-looking bed that Armstrong mentioned, just on the other side of the wire. Matt is reluctant to follow the shape of the bed across to its end and to the floor, where Armstrong told them the body was. He has to though; there is no getting away from it, no matter how strong his feeling of dread at seeing the body.

There in the shadows, curled up as if it was asleep, is the outline of a naked human. Matt cannot see much detail from his angle, but he can see that the body is male and despite not having any view of the face, its features look ominously familiar.

Matt's head spins and his eyes blur as the blood drains from his brain. He suddenly feels as if he could pass out.

Matt has no option other than to drop to his haunches before he keels over. He hears voices talking to him as he puts his head between his knees in an attempt to get some blood pumping back into his brain.

"Are you okay?" Matt finally hears Armstrong ask, as the arteries in the back of his neck pulse, bringing his starving brain some fresh oxygen.

"Yes, I'm fine. Sorry... I went a bit faint for a second there," Matt replies, his vision returning and his breathing equalising.

"Don't worry, it's understandable," Armstrong reassures as he helps Matt back to his feet.

"Is it my dad?" Matt asks.

"We don't know that yet. The cage door is padlocked and the face is out of view. I'm afraid you will need to identify him if you're up to it," Armstrong asks.

"I'll be okay now; I'm just not used to it."

"You never are, not really," Armstrong says. "Is there a hammer and a chisel, so we can get the padlock open? Fleck has called for an ambulance but we have to check if we can offer assistance. It can make all the difference."

"Yes, I think my dad's toolbox it under his desk, so I'll check," Matt says, turning.

The toolbox is indeed under the desk and Matt gets out a hammer and a chisel and gives them to Armstrong. Without delay, Armstrong takes them over to the cage door, repositions the padlock and places the chisel on top of it. After one slow swing of the hammer to take aim, Armstrong lifts it again and then whacks the hammer into the head of the chisel. The padlock snaps open all too easily, its body clattering to the floor.

"Just hold back please, Matt," Armstrong tells Matt again as he puts the tools down on the floor. Fleck, who still seems unaffected by anything that's occurred so far, kicks the padlock's body to the side and unhooks the shackle off the cage door. She looks at Armstrong, waiting for his say-so to proceed. He nods his approval for her to open the door, his face deadly serious.

Chapter 13

The square wired panel rattles in the steel frame of the cage door as it knocks into the wired wall behind it, and the door finally opens. Armstrong and Fleck don't rush in to check the body's pulse, however; they go in slowly, deliberately, their training and experience put to full use.

Armstrong knows all too well to expect the unexpected, as does Fleck, but this room has been locked up for all but two weeks. He is not expecting to find any signs of life, no matter what Matt's overactive imagination heard in the dark last night.

The two officers stand over the curled-up body, whose arm is flopped across his head, hiding his face. They look for any sign of weapons or other possible dangers before they close in on the body, finding there isn't anything.

"Check for a pulse," Armstrong orders Fleck, not that he expects she will find one, judging by the colourless skin the body is displaying.

"I'll toss you for it, Boss?" Fleck says.

"And why would I do that? You know what they say?"

"What do they say?" Fleck asks and immediately regrets it.

"Shit rolls downhill," Armstrong tells her, grinning.

"Yea, right, for fuck's sake," Fleck moans in defeat as she magically produces a pair of latex gloves from her pocket and pulls them on. Bending down, her index and middle fingers are poised to try and find a pulse on the body's neck.

Matt can see from Armstrong's grimace that he is relieved to be able to delegate the task to Fleck, almost recoiling when Fleck's fingers reach the body's neck.

"The body is cold," Fleck observes when she touches it at arm's length.

"Is there a pulse?" Armstrong asks.

Fleck is silent for a moment while her fingers probe the neck area just below the body's jawline. "Afraid not, Boss, no pulse," she informs him, glancing in Matt's direction.

"Okay, carefully move his arm away from his face, so we can see who it is," Armstrong orders.

Fleck obeys without question, and with the same hand, again at arm's length, she takes hold of the wrist and pulls the arm down and away from the face. The head is at an odd angle against the floor, turned up with the face pointed towards the ceiling.

Both officers are taken aback by the face's chilling, contorted features, its eyes fixed open wide, instilling fear into them both, even though they are both very familiar with dead people's faces.

Fleck, who is closer, is transfixed by the wide, merciless eyes that have big black pupils staring at the nothingness above. She blinks, trying to break the spell in which she is caught, but when her eyes open, the dead eyes are staring directly into hers. Terror rips through Fleck, her confusion absolute. How can a dead man's eyes move?

She goes to stand, to put space between the evil staring at her, but her legs are slow to react. They have gone numb, the blood having been forced out of them by their low, bent position.

Fleck's panic escalates out of control as the face around the eyes creases, its muscles moving to open its mouth. Disgusting yellow teeth appear behind the face's narrow, black, dried-out lips, and then the head begins to rise from the floor. Fleck's terror has her vision fixed upon the hideous face moving in her direction, and she doesn't see the clawed hand that has also awakened, its arm reaching for her.

Fleck's unresponsive legs have failed to push her up fully, and she is caught in a stooping position when the hand grips onto her ankle. She tries to scream but the outburst is caught in her throat by her terror, her legs giving way. She falls backwards, hitting the bed behind her. She kicks out violently in panic, trying to free her ankle, but the grip tightens and her leg is pulled away from her.

Armstrong is stunned for a moment, not believing his eyes as the 'dead' body moves and goes to attack Fleck, its grizzly mouth gaping open, attempting to bite down onto Fleck's leg. Quickly regaining some composure, Armstrong strikes out at the undead body with his foot, kicking at it, his foot crunching into the ribcage of the creature. The blow has no effect despite the breaking bones he is sure his kick inflicted into the ribs where his foot hit.

Armstrong quickly changes tactics and aims another kick, this time at the undead creature's head, putting as much force into the kick as he can muster. The kick is strong, his foot smashing into the back of the creature's head. Pain flares in Armstrong's foot from the collision, making him wince, but the kick whips the head right at Fleck's leg.

Fleck's frenzied attempt to scramble away from the teeth gnashing at her leg are desperate, every fibre within her recoiling, but the head suddenly shoots forward, banging straight into her. Now, Fleck does scream as the hand tightens again around her ankle, and searing pain explodes from her calf. Dead teeth tear into her muscle, ripping through the material covering her leg that offers no protection from the disgusting yellow teeth. She screams again hysterically as the teeth close around her flesh, and the creature's head pulls away, taking its chunk of meat with it. Blood sprays out of the wound, splattering across the creature's face to join the smeared red blood around its chomping mouth.

Stunned, Armstrong watches the creature bite into Fleck, her scream ripping into his eardrums. The head pulls away from Fleck's legs as blood sprays and Armstrong kicks again, this time into the retreating face of the beast, his foot crushing its nose. This time, he gets the result he wanted and the creature shoots backwards away from his partner, who bolts from the creature's grip, scrambling out of the cage door on all fours.

Matt, who stands outside, paralyzed in disbelief, sees Fleck break loose and finally, he goes to help her escape. She comes flying out of the cage, however, adrenaline pushing her off her hands and into a low sprint away from the danger. Fleck's sprint is out of control and she collides with Matt, knocking him sideways before she stumbles and crashes headfirst into the wall next to the basement stairs. Matt's back hits the side wall as Fleck goes down with a sickening thud. She doesn't get up off the floor.

Armstrong moves to get out of the cage and to close the door on the undead creature that has just taken a bite out of Fleck. He sees her crash into the wall and looks down in astonishment, his concern for her desperate, seeing she isn't moving.

Bolts of pain shoot through his foot when he applies pressure to it. He can only hope his bones are badly bruised and not broken from lashing out at the creature, and he stumbles through the wired doorway.

Behind Armstrong, slithering around on the floor, the zombie that was once named Jonathan Bradley feels the fresh human meat drop into its stomach. Its belly welcomes the meat it craves, rewarding the creature by sending unknown chemicals coursing through its body. These empower the creature, revitalising every muscle they find, willing the creature on to find even more juicy flesh to consume. In an instant, the zombie manoeuvres itself into a crouching position, and it pounces at lightning speed at its next prey.

Matt sees the creature jump, its speed too fast to warn Armstrong of the impending, terrifying threat. But in that instant, Matt sees, he sees the face of his father. His grotesque transformation is not enough to mask Matt's recognition that hits him like a thunderbolt.

Matt is once more frozen in disbelief and fear as his father lands on Armstrong's back, knocking him forward and off his feet.

A cry of shock escapes Armstrong's mouth as he goes down, the creature clinging on around his neck, its mouth already gaping, ready to feed.

Armstrong hits the ground heavily, his fall only broken by the bloodied legs of Fleck who hasn't moved an inch since crashing into the wall.

The pile of bodies next to the stairs writhes around as Armstrong tries to save himself from the creature on top of him. His elbows shoot back, trying to hit the creature off him, and his back bucks, but Armstrong is pinned down and the creature's need to feed again is relentless.

"Matt, help…" Armstrong pleads.

Matt pushes himself off the wall against which he landed, quickly going to pick up the hammer Armstrong discarded on the floor, after knocking the padlock apart. His hand closes around the handle and he turns to face Armstrong who struggles for his life.

As Matt contemplates using the hammer as a weapon against his father, a deathly groan rises from the other side of the room. The head of the beast is buried in the side of

Armstrong's neck, the head wriggling from side to side as it bites into the doomed police officer.

Matt is too late, and all he can do is watch as Armstrong is fed upon, the creature satisfying its gnawing hunger for flesh. But can its hunger be satisfied, Matt suddenly thinks?

Panic rises deep within Matt as he realises he is trapped in his father's lair, the zombie's lair. Bodies block the stairs, and there is no way past, short of climbing over the back of the beast as it feeds. Matt cannot reach the stairs.

Would his dad attack him as he has the police officers? Would the crazed creature even recognise its own son, its flesh and blood? The words *flesh and blood* stick in Matt's head—even as he struggles to work out if he would be considered prey by the creature—as his mind scrambles to find a way out. His intuition tells him he would indeed be no more than a new source of flesh for the beast, and his hand tightens on the handle of the hammer.

Matt instinctively knows that there is only one way out for him, and that he has to fight, has to use the hammer to kill the beast.

And he has to do it now, while it is distracted eating Armstrong.

The decision made, Matt goes to move forward, ignoring the terrifying fear within him, but the creature's head suddenly stops wriggling and rises away from Armstrong's neck. *Has the creature read my thoughts? Is my father still in there somewhere?* Matt thinks suddenly, rooted to the spot again. *Don't be ridiculous, strike now, while you can,* he tells himself. But he is too late, as his element of surprise is gone.

The beast's head turns, inching around in Matt's direction, its piercing evil eyes leading the way. Blood drips from the chin of the creature that has Matt's father's features, its tongue lapping at its lips, finding the blood it craves. Matt is motionless, staring into the beast's eyes, looking for any small sign that the beast recognises him—even as his terror builds. There is no sign of his father; he is gone, lost to the creature staring at him, the creature that quickly moves to climb off the bodies it is perched upon.

Matt realises, horrified, that the creature's craving to feed is burning within it, and that he is next on its menu. There is no place to hide from its baying teeth, but there is one chance of survival, the cage behind Matt.

His dad designed it to lock Wendy in, but can it lock the beast out?

Matt steps back to retreat into his only possible salvation, but the creature is already standing upright, poised to attack.

Matt knows he has left it too late. He backs away, hitting the cage's wire as the beast moves to strike. Matt suddenly remembers the hammer—his weapon—in his hand and goes to raise it.

A leg kicks up from the floor below the beast as it bursts into action, and tangles with its legs, tripping it, making it fall to the floor. This time, Matt doesn't delay. He spins to the side, rushing into the cage, grabbing the door as he goes and pulling it until it slams shut. In a split second, the beast springs up off the floor and crashes into the closed wired door of the cage that clatters heavily in its frame.

Fear forces Matt back and away from the door, as the creature clings onto it through the mesh, its anger spiralling. Its eyes pierce into Matt as it pushes against the door, trying to force it in, but it can't. Matt's ears ring as a high-pitched screech rings out from the depths of the beast's throat, its mouth gaping until it suddenly stops and the beast calms down slightly.

Cowering against the opposite wall, Matt's relief that the door is strong enough to hold the creature back immediately turns to panic again as the beast's pressure against the door relaxes. Matt sees the door open a tiny amount as weight is taken off it, and it abruptly dawns on him that nothing is stopping the door from swinging back open.

Think, Matt, think, he shouts in his head hysterically, dreading that the beast will quickly come to the same conclusion about the door. Forcing himself, Matt takes a step forward towards the door, and immediately, the beast reacts, pushing forward, its face's skin seeping into the mesh in its overriding desperation to feed.

The beast quickly relaxes again, and the door moves outwards a sliver under its own weight, and then a thought pops into Matt's head. He steps forward again, tempting the beast towards the mesh that is only inches away from him.

Matt directs his eyes away from the hideous monster in front of him as drool from its mouth intertwines with the wire. He looks down at the claw of the hammer, then to the square wire in front of him. Before the beast can react, Matt pushes the claw through the closest square of wire to the doorframe, and pulls the hammer in the opposite direction away from the door. The claw hooks around the frame, catching against the outside of the door, locking it into position. As long as he keeps pressure on the handle of the hammer, it should stop the door from opening outwards. Matt is confident the claw will hold the door closed, but to test his theory, he carefully reaches down to a section of the door that is free from the beast, and he pushes it gently. The door stays rigidly closed, locked into place by the hammer.

Moving to the side, relieved that he is secure despite the ferocious monster close by, Matt goes to sit on the end of the bed to figure out his next move, his hand gripping the hammer firmly. But before he can sit, something moves at the other end of the basement and a figure rises slowly from the floor, from under the body of Armstrong. Fleck, Matt sees with relief, has woken and is getting to her feet. Thankfully, she must have come around after banging her head.

Matt nearly shouts out to her, to tell her that he is in the cage, but he catches himself just in time. He must keep the beast's attention on him and away from her. She must escape up the stairs, escape, and bring help. Matt distracts the creature at the door by rattling the wire mesh, sending it into a frenzy, but keeping its focus on him, at the same time shouting out to Fleck.

She stands with her back to him, not moving for a moment, not acknowledging his calls. Is she concussed or just drowsy from the blow to her head, Matt thinks, confused? “Fleck,” Matt shouts again, “I need help. Go back upstairs, get to safety and find help.”

The creature behind the wire is going crazy; it claws at the mesh, searching for a way through, its fingernails scraping over the wire, cracking and snapping them. But it doesn't relent. “Fleck,” Matt shouts desperately once more, and finally, the police officer turns, striking yet more fear into Matt's racked body, her face contorted, gruesome, just like his father's.

At Fleck's feet, Armstrong's dead body suddenly begins to fit wildly, his entire body jerking uncontrollably. Without warning, Fleck rushes forward, straight at Matt, and she smashes into the wire with such a force that the crash rings out, bouncing off the basement walls. Matt ducks in reflex, fearing the wire will split and give way, his hand nearly slipping from the hammer's handle which is slick with his sweat. Dust rains down from above as the cage's fixings are jolted by the tremendous force, but they hold and the wire doesn't split.

Two ferocious creatures bay for Matt's blood, each one snarling and screeching, clawing at the wire frantically to feed on his flesh. Another is yet to join them; Armstrong, too, has reanimated into an undead zombie, the side of his neck in bloody tatters, eaten away.

He stands behind his brethren, ominously watching over the proceedings, ignoring their hideous noise as he waits for the sound of human prey.

Only silence comes from Matt now. No help will be offered to him by the wretched creatures, no matter who they were in their previous lives. His hand aches on the handle of the hammer with the amount of force it takes to hold it secure, and not even his mind racing to compute what is happening can mask the dull throb. He swaps hands, not only to relieve the ache, but also to get his phone out of his pocket. He needs to find help somewhere else.

Thinking for a moment before opening his phone, Matt can't decide who he should call. Should he phone the police? And tell them what, that their officers have been attacked by an undead creature and turned into zombies themselves? Firstly, they will think he is a lunatic who has gone off his meds, and secondly, won't they just despatch more officers to suffer the same fate as Armstrong and Fleck?

No matter how scared Matt is and how uncomfortable he may be, he doesn't want his father's lunacy to cause more terrifying slaughter by dragging other officers into his basement. Wendy, however, could go into the local police station and explain the situation fully. She is in town and close to the police station now. They will probably think she has gone mad too, but she would have more chance to convince them and insist that they take precautions, whatever they may be.

Matt quickly makes the call to Wendy but he is met immediately with her voicemail. *Damn it!* he thinks and leaves her a garbled message to phone him as soon as possible. As a backup of sorts, he also sends her a text message telling her the same. He can only hope that she isn't as remiss with her phone today as she has been, by her own admission, lately.

She is expecting his call to update her, so she will surely be checking her phone sooner rather than later, Matt hopes.

Forced to swap hands again, as the now familiar ache spreads into his other hand, Matt tells himself that he can hold out where he is for as long as it takes for Wendy to receive his messages and phone him back. He tries to sit quietly and calmly despite his racing heart. The less movement and noise he makes, the less the creatures make, and the more placid they become. Matt needs to keep them placid; he doesn't know how much more of their ferocious behaviour he can stand. His ears are already ringing from their incessant high-pitched screeching that knows no bounds.

Chapter 14

More than half an hour has passed since Matt tried to reach Wendy, and he has tried several more times to reach her since. He is beginning to wonder if she has forgotten her phone and forgotten him. Using his time constructively, Matt has managed to bring himself some relief. The hammer is now held in place by his belt. He's secured the belt around the hammer's handle, and then tied it off to the wire of the cage, pulling it taut.

The basement is relatively quiet, apart from the constant grunts and snarls made by all three of the creatures, but you could cut the atmosphere with a knife. Almost any movement or noise Matt makes riles the creatures up again, and they seem to feed off his energy and the promise of fresh meat it offers.

With the hammer secured, Matt inches his way from the mesh as far as possible on the bed, and then he moves back steadily on the bed until he can lean his back against the wall.

Fleck, her face pressed up hard against the wire, watches him creep away but hardly reacts. Once he has rested his back against the wall, her face leaves the wire until gradually, her whole body leaves the wire completely. She now stands a couple of feet back, her head dropped forward as if she has fallen into a stupor.

The beast that is his father follows Matt across, once Fleck makes way. It crawls along the mesh, its hands virtually pulling it along. One after the other, they slowly leave the mesh, only to land on it again a few inches across, its fingers curling through to pull it across.

The beast is now level with where Matt is sitting, its eyes peering through the squares of the wire, watching him intently. Matt is convinced that somewhere in its dead head, the beast has some form of recognition for Matt.

Matt can't help but peer back at the creature with a wave of anger burning in his stomach. How could his father have done what he did to Wendy, to torture, rape and feed her poison, and then abduct a young girl off the street, planning to inflict the same on her? *Well, you got your comeuppance, didn't you, Father!*

"Fuck you, Dad!" Matt whispers to his father deliberately, his face full of hatred and anger.

You may be a monster now, Matt thinks, *but you were an even worse one before. At least everyone can see you for what you really are now, an evil fucking depraved monster.*

Matt has to turn away from the creature; it is too upsetting to look at it any longer. He feels its eyes on him though, watching and waiting. *Perhaps it will be his biggest victory,* Matt ponders, *to feed on his own son and turn him into an undead zombie! Well, fuck you; you're not my father any longer, and I'll bury that hammer deep into your head before I let you turn me into one of you. I am nothing like you!*

Matt's heartbreak is stifling. His father, his closest friend when he was little, has morphed into pure evil, and that was before Wendy got the better of him against all the odds and bit him. She has paid Bradley back in spades, with the very poison he fed her, but what a shame that poison hasn't just killed him instead of turning him into a monster that has attacked two other people.

Suddenly, Matt's head turns up to the ceiling. Does he hear a muffled voice from upstairs, or is it his imagination? The voice sounds again, a female, and footsteps vibrate through the floor and into the basement. *Shit, somebody is in the house. Is it Wendy?* Matt panics. *Keep quiet,* he tells himself, *don't draw her into the basement... But Wendy will come down for sure, but then it might not be her!*

Matt's mind races; if it is Wendy, he has to shout out to try and warn her of the danger and tell her to get out. But if it's not her, shouting out will only bring whoever it is into the basement. The creatures are still quiet, and don't seem to have noticed the new noises from upstairs, but how long will that last? *Fucking hell!* Matt's mind screams, he doesn't know what to do, *keep quiet*, he tells himself, *it can't be Wendy, she is in town. Why would she come here without phoning me first? Keep quiet and whoever it is will see no one is home, and leave.*

The pad of footsteps continues and Matt realises that there is more than one person making them. *Go away, stay out of the basement,* he pleads, trying to remember if the basement door is open or closed.

Another voice sounds out from above, a male one, and this time, the voice is clearly audible, as it calls out Armstrong's name. Armstrong's head whips around in the direction of the stairs, his body tensing, ready to attack. "Armstrong!" the voice shouts again, and now the other two beasts hear it. Fleck jolts out of her stupor, turning in the same direction as Armstrong, and Bradley's head turns slightly towards the sound.

The beast's eyes, however, inexplicably don't shift from staring at Matt.

WPC Gardener sees the basement door ajar and assumes that it must be where Detective Armstrong is. He isn't anywhere else in the house after all, and he has to be in here somewhere, otherwise, why would his car be parked across the driveway with the front door on the catch? The detective might need backup, which is why her partner, WPC Miller, pulled up behind Armstrong's car to let herself and PC Cross check out the situation.

Cross comes back down the stairs, his hi-vis patrol vest snugly fitted to his hulking chest and almost blinding Gardener, just as she is about to go and investigate the basement.

"All quiet up there," Cross tells Gardener. "You check out the basement while I radio it in. There's something strange going on here."

"Definitely something fishy going on," Gardener agrees as her hand reaches for the basement door. "Armstrong," she says as the door opens.

Armstrong's name hits Matt's ears as clear as a bell. The female voice is not Wendy's and he watches in hopeless dread as Armstrong bolts into the stairwell and then Fleck rushes towards it, their deafening shrieks of the hunt echoing around the basement as they go.

Matt, on the spur of the moment, reaches forward to touch Bradley's disgusting fingers, poking through the wire. He cannot stop the other two beasts from attacking whoever is looking for Armstrong, but maybe he can keep one of the creatures with him, although he doesn't know if it will make a difference to the poor buggers above.

Matt puts his fingers on top of Bradley's. "Dad," he says, revolted, "stay with me. Don't go away and leave me here alone." Matt keeps talking to the wretched beast, telling him all kinds of bullshit to try and keep him from following the other two creatures and attacking the people who have wandered into this hellscape. And Matt's ploy works, as Bradley's hideous eyes stay on his and he doesn't move from the mesh, despite the horrendous sounds of carnage seeping down into the basement from above.

"Armstrong?" Gardener repeats weakly and unsure, her hand wavering on the door as the deathly screams reverberate up the stairwell. Shadows move as something rushes up the stairs, and Gardener looks over to Cross for support. His mouth is stuck open next to his radio, fear etched on his face.

Panicked by the chilling screams and oncoming shadows, Gardener steps back, her arm pushing the door closed. Whatever it is coming up those stairs, she wants no part of it. It's definitely better to wait for the backup Cross is requesting. Her hand moves to the door handle as it closes, and she waits for the click to confirm it is fully shut.

No click sounds and Gardener is flung backwards as the door bursts open with a tremendous force, her back crashing into the wall behind her, the blow taking her breath away. A figure rushes at her through the doorway and she quickly raises her arms to try and stop the perpetrator from hitting into her. She does manage to catch the person for a moment. Gardener's arms begin to buckle immediately under the weight, as her eyes finally focus on her attacker. She barely has time to register the fear that the grotesque-looking monster attacking her instils deep within her as she fights to keep it at bay.

Cross watches in shocked disbelief as Gardener is pinned against the wall by her attacker. The attacker is Armstrong, Cross is sure of it, but his face is twisted and crazed, his mouth gaping open as if he wants to bite into Gardener. *What the fuck!* Cross thinks as Armstrong snarls into Gardener's face as he goes to pull Armstrong off her and see what the hell is going on with him.

Before Cross has a chance to pull the two police officers apart, another person bursts out of the basement door and crashes into the back of Armstrong, the blow causing Gardener's arms to fold. Gardener's scream rips into Cross as Armstrong inexplicably buries his face into the side of

Gardener's, then immediately pulls his head away, tearing her cheek away with him.

Gardener's shocked and terrified face turns to Cross, her eyes desperately pleading for his help, blood pouring from the wound on the side of her face where her cheek once was. Cross goes to move again, to help Gardener, but the other person is blocking his path and he has to move his focus to them as Armstrong's head buries itself into the side of Gardener's neck.

Cross thinks he is tripping for a second as he looks at Detective Fleck's contorted face.

She stands in front of him, crouched over, poised to attack him, her mouth snarling and her hands like claws.

"Calm down, Fleck; what is going on?" Cross says uselessly, as he tries to stare down her evil eyes.

Fleck answers Cross's question with a deafening screech from her cavernous hole of a mouth as she takes a step forward and jumps at him. Cross is not prepared for Fleck to attack him; all he can do is raise an arm to fend off his fellow police officer and his white shirt sleeve offers no protection from the teeth that sink into his arm.

Gardener falls to the floor in front of Cross as Fleck's teeth bite down into his arm, blood immediately staining his freshly laundered shirt. Cross's disbelief is quickly overridden by his need to fight and defend himself, and he finally puts those muscles that he has spent so much time honing, to use. His body whips around as his other arm grabs hold of Fleck's midriff and he slams Fleck into the door frame of the kitchen next to him. Her back smashes into the frame with a sickening crunch, and she falls to the ground, but not without taking her chunk of flesh from Cross's arm with her.

Cross's eyes stare at the stained hole in his shirt sleeve and the bloody serrated wound below it in horror for a second, anger welling inside him. A hand grabs hold of his trouser leg, pulling Cross out of his momentary trance just in time to see Fleck's head go forward to take another bite out of him, this time out of his leg. Cross yanks his leg back and out of her mouth's vicinity, and then he kicks the leg forward, smashing his foot into Fleck's face. Fleck's head is rocketed backwards, taking her body with it, and she ends up in a pile on the floor just inside the kitchen.

Gardener! Cross suddenly thinks, staring down at Fleck's squirming body as he turns towards her. *Shit, no.* His mind races as he sees Gardener down on the floor, blood pooling around her, and Armstrong crouched over the body, his head buried into her stomach area. Not willing to leave her like this, Cross grabs his telescopic baton from the utility belt fitted around his waist. Taking a step forward, he deliberately whips the baton through the air and it extends to its full length with a satisfying snap.

Armstrong's head springs up from Gardener's blood-soaked belly at the sound of the baton's snap, his terrifying, threatening face, warning Cross to stay back from his prize. Undeterred, Cross takes another step forward as Armstrong's blood-smeared mouth swallows the meat into his gullet.

"Get away from her, Armstrong, you fucker!" Cross spits at the detective.

Armstrong pushes himself up further, his arms depressing into Gardener's chest, his soaked lips parting to show Cross his red-stained teeth—through which sickly bubbles grow—as he hisses at Cross.

Cross's fear rises uncontrollably inside him at Armstrong's hideous display, and he falters in his advance; the creature sees Cross's fear written all over his face. Cross feels Armstrong's body tense up, terror overriding any thoughts of attacking the beast as Cross realises that the tables have suddenly been turned, and now Cross is about to become the victim.

In the split second that Armstrong springs off Gardener's body to attack his new prey, Cross turns and bolts for the front door. His only thought is that he has left it too late to escape. He sees, thankfully, that the front door is still three-quarters of the way open, and he reaches for it even as the creature behind flies through the air at him. Only Cross's instinct makes him duck down low at the perfect time to let the creature fly over his shoulders and ducked head.

The beast squeals wildly in anger as it misses its prey and smashes heavily into the solid wall behind the front door, and Cross swings the door open to hit the creature again, trapping it for vital seconds. Parked exactly where it was when Cross got out, the brightly marked police car is close when he exits the house, its blue lights flashing in the dark evening sky as a warning to other drivers. WPC Miller sits behind the wheel tapping on her phone, oblivious to the horrific carnage taking place.

Another terrifying screech accosts Cross's ears as he careers out of the house, the creature now scrambling to regain its footing to attack again; Cross knows it without having to look back. He sprints to the passenger door in only a few strides, banging against it, desperate to take advantage of the refuge the car offers and yanking at the door handle.

WPC Miller's finger hovers in mid-air above her phone screen as the sudden commotion arriving from nowhere startles her.

"What the fuck!" she exclaims as Cross drops into the passenger seat and slams the door closed.

"Drive!" he shouts at her without ceremony as he watches Armstrong race down the driveway after him.

"Where's Chris?" Miller asks, referring to Christine Gardener, her partner.

"She's dead. Now fucking drive before we are too," Cross shouts.

"Dead?" Miller asks, alarmed, making no movement to drive in her confusion, her finger still hovering in the air. Only now is she noticing the blood pouring from Cross's arm. "What..."

Before Miller can ask her question, the passenger side window implodes, raining lumps of glass over Cross and sprinkling them over Miller. Armstrong's head is suddenly next to Cross, its torrid face only inches away, gnashing teeth preparing to bite. Cross raises his bloodied arm again to defend himself, and manages to hook the creature under its chin with his forearm and force its head away until it is pinned against the upper frame of the window. Remnants of glass in the frame slice and crunch into the back of the creature's neck and Cross pushes again in the hopes it will disable the beast.

"Drive!" Cross shouts again as he continues to force the creature into the glass, but no matter how hard he pushes, it doesn't stop the creature's teeth from gnashing at him.

With the engine already running, Miller, in shock, does as she is told. She crunches the gearbox into reverse, backs up a few meters, and then shoves the gearbox into first. The police car's wheels lose their grip for a second, screeching against the road until they suddenly bite and the car lurches forward. Miller swerves into the road around the other parked, unmarked police car with Armstrong hanging from the passenger window.

Cross strains to hold the creature in position against the window frame as Miller speeds away from the house, but somehow, he still manages to see Fleck at the open doorway of the house as they go past. He could easily release the beast now and let it fall into the road, but that would only release it onto the public where it would cause untold slaughter. Fleck is beyond his control right now, but the city centre is only a short distance away, where Armstrong would have his pick from the throngs of late-night Christmas shoppers to feed upon.

"Get us back to the station," Cross pleads urgently.

“What the hell is happening?” Miller insists.

Cross cannot answer her; his strength is suddenly beginning to wane. The strain is too much, he tells himself as stars appear before his eyes. Despite the size of the muscles in his arm, it is on fire and the pain is emanating from the wound on his forearm. The burning agony is quickly spreading down his arm, through his chest and into his stomach, his hold on Armstrong about to fail. Cross doesn’t want to think about what is causing the burning agony. He desperately looks out of the car to see where they are. He sees that they are just coming upon the shopping centre, where the police station is situated. Miller will be turning anytime now to take them around the back and into the station’s car park.

“Aaaaah,” Cross screams out as the pain becomes too much to bear and he buckles over in the passenger seat, the fire ignited throughout his entire body.

Armstrong’s undead body falls away from the speeding police car and into the road, hitting the tarmac hard and tumbling over until it skids to a stop right at the entrance to the pedestrian area of the shopping centre. Onlookers gasp in surprise and fright as the tattered body comes to a stop, and do-gooders hurry over to offer their assistance to the injured man.

Luckily for the casualty, he has landed close to an ambulance that has set up for the day next to the shopping centre, to offer medical care to shoppers who find their Christmas shopping expedition has taken its toll on them. Two paramedics donned out in Father Christmas hats professionally take charge of the situation, but quickly wish they hadn’t…

Miller slams on the car’s brakes, stopping the car close by as the body falls into the road, Cross looks as if he is in need of the hospital and not the police station. She leans over to check on him, although she cannot see much as he is bent right over in his seat.

"Tom are you okay? What's wrong?" Miller asks, concerned. Cross doesn't answer. *Perhaps he has lost a lot of blood?* Miller wonders as she grabs his shoulder and tries to sit him upright.

A cold breeze blows through the shattered window next to Cross, but his body is ice cold to the touch, Miller feels through his shirt as she touches his arm. *He can't have lost that much blood that it's dropped his temperature that much,* Miller thinks as she pulls at him again, getting worried that he could have another injury she hasn't noticed.

To her relief, Cross, with her help, begins to come up from his bent over position and she pulls him harder to help, until he flops back onto his seat. *Shit!* she thinks when she sees his face. It has lost all colour, so he must be in a bad way. Putting her hand on his chest, her concern grows when she doesn't feel him breathing and she goes to move her hand to his neck to see if he has a pulse.

Like a shot and with his eyes still closed, Cross's hand shoots up and grabs hers disturbingly, just as it leaves his chest. "Stop messing around," Miller tells him, but she feels no humour in Cross's tight, cold grip. "Let me go," she yells as she tries to pull her arm away, but he doesn't. His grip tightens around her wrist.

"Tom, you're hurting me, stop it now." Miller yanks her arm, his vice-like grip only tightening again, the pressure on her bones flexing them, threatening to snap and crush them completely.

Cross's eyes snap open, shocking Miller, her attention drawn away from the pain in her wrist by their strange lifeless appearance, her dread at his behaviour mounting. "How are you feeling?" she asks, feebly trying to sound concerned for his wellbeing and to garner his favour in the hope he will release her. Her words fall flat, as his grip remains, and it begins to pull her closer to him across the car. She is powerless to resist his colossal strength.

Miller's other arm strains against the back of Cross's seat, pushing back to try and counter the irresistible force pulling her across the car. Her attempt is futile, so her body is dragged over, her fear turning to terror when Cross's head turns in her direction. His lifeless face creases into evil as his mouth opens, and it dawns on Miller that Armstrong has bitten Cross's arm, and now Cross means to bite into *her* flesh.

Releasing the back of the seat as she realises she is in a fight for her life, Miller lashes out with her free hand. Her nails dig into the side of Cross's face, her fingers closing around the soft skin around Cross's left eye. Cross closes the eye to protect himself but Miller doesn't relent. She feels the join of his eyelid and pushes her middle finger into it as hard as she can.

Deep gurgling noises emanate from Cross's gaping mouth that is now so close to Miller's shoulder, his teeth primed to sink into it. Miller doesn't know if the noise is caused by the pain she is inflicting on his eye, but she has no other defence to make, and she pushes her finger again. Her finger sinks into the damp eye socket past her second knuckle, and she feels the eyeball squeezed next to her finger.

Miller's back fights to hold its position, every fibre in her body straining to stop the teeth from touching her as her finger curls around the back of Cross's eyeball. Pressure and then shooting pain erupt in Miller's shoulder as Cross's teeth pierce through her skin. She screams out in agony, her finger hooking around Cross's eyeball and she rips her hand back.

Cross bites deep into Miller's shoulder, the agony is so excruciating that she doesn't notice the eyeball she has ripped out of Cross's head. It slips through her fingers to hang by its nerves, and it now bobbles against her face as the beast feeds on her arm.

A knock on Miller's window goes unanswered. She has passed out from the pain, succumbed entirely to the creature feeding upon her, and it gorges itself on the warm, wet meat, filling its belly. Another knock sounds, more impatient now, but still the caller is ignored. Undeterred, they bend down to peer through the glass to see why the police officers are ignoring them, their hands reaching for the door handle.

Chapter 15

She is such a lovely girl, Wendy thinks as Emma listens avidly to her explanation of what happened to them both at the hands of Wendy's disturbed and estranged husband. Wendy keeps her voice low so that nobody overhears her sad story. Not that anyone is interested; everyone in the busy coffee shop is too engrossed in their own problems and just happy to be able to take a break from their hectic day of Christmas shopping

Emma's face changes constantly as she listens to Wendy talk. Expressions of disbelief and shock are common, but Emma's face ultimately conveys pity and sadness for Wendy as the trauma to which she was subjected unfolds. Emma listens in silence, for the most part, sipping her coffee, and only occasionally does she ask the odd question or speak to convey her support for Wendy.

Wendy tells Emma all that she knows about her abduction, which isn't much, but she tells her every detail about the struggle to escape from Bradley's capture. Wendy can see that Emma's feelings are growing angry as she tells her of the beating Bradley inflicted on her. Those feelings change to relief and satisfaction, Wendy notices as she talks about Bradley's ultimate defeat. She also notices the underlying shock Emma has when she hears of how Wendy did eventually win her success.

Her head dropping, Wendy apologises profusely for not having the strength to tell Emma what had happened to them and for lying to her, telling her that she couldn't remember.

"You don't owe me an apology, Wendy," Emma says with a tear in her eye. "If it wasn't for you, he would have done the same to me as he did to you. You saved me, Wendy, and I will be forever grateful to you for that."

"I couldn't let him do that to you," Wendy says, reaching across the table to put her hand on Emma's. "I would've died before I left you there, in his clutches."

"I know you would have and thank you. I only wish he hadn't put you through so much."

"It's in the past now, and I have got to try and put it behind me. What else can I do?" Wendy says, trying to sound at least a bit positive.

"You're very brave, but if you need to talk about it, anytime, I'm here for you," Emma says sincerely.

"Thank you, Emma, that means a lot to me."

"Can I get you anything else, another coffee?" a waitress asks, arriving beside the table.

"Another drink, Emma?" Wendy asks.

"No thank you. I should be going; my parents will be waiting for me. I've been longer than I thought I would be."

"I'll have another coffee please," Wendy tells the waitress, who takes the order and moves on.

"Thank you for meeting with me and telling me what happened," Emma says.

"Not at all, I should have done it sooner."

"It has put my mind at ease, to know what happened to me. It will be a relief for my parents to know what happened that night too; they have been very worried," Emma says, picking up her handbag and preparing to go.

"I should think they have."

"Will you let me know what happens with the police when you hear, please?" Emma asks.

"Yes, of course, I will. I'm sure someone will phone me soon. I thought they would have been here by now, Detective Armstrong wanted to speak to you. He will have to phone you if you have to go. Are you going straight home?"

"No, not straight away. I've got to pick a couple of things up from the shops while I'm here, but I won't be long, hopefully."

"Well, good luck," Wendy says, looking out at the crowds through the window, "I think you're going to need it. It's very busy out there."

"Oh God, I know, I hate Christmas shopping," Emma says, getting up from her chair and picking up her coat.

"You and me both," Wendy says, getting up with her.

Emma puts on her coat and comes around the table to hug Wendy and say goodbye.

"Thank you again," Emma says.

"Please, there is no need to keep thanking me, it's the least I could do. He was my husband after all."

"Don't blame yourself, Wendy." Emma smiles. "He was clearly deranged, which isn't your fault. Phone me when you hear, okay?"

"Of course, and please say hello to your parents for me."

Wendy watches as Emma leaves to join the masses outside. She doesn't envy her in the slightest. It's dark, cold and rammed with people out there, and no amount of Christmas carols will make the experience any better.

As Wendy takes her seat again to wait for her coffee, of which there is no sign yet, she decides to give Matt a call to see how he is getting on. He must know something by now. Her arm reaches around to the back of her chair to find the pocket in her coat into which she put her phone.

"One coffee, Madam. Is there anything else I can get you?" the waitress asks, surprising Wendy just as her hand feels her phone.

"No thanks, just the bill."

"Certainly," the waitress replies and walks off. Wendy unlocks her phone's screen as her coffee steams away in front of her. A rush of panic hits her when her screen lights up. *Shit,* she thinks, as she sees how many phone calls she has missed from Matt and that there are several voicemails and messages waiting for her to read, all from him. *Why didn't the bloody thing ring?* she thinks, but she quickly notices that the phone is set to silent for some reason and she feels her stupidity for not double-checking it.

Quickly clicking onto the first text message, she feels her stupidity deepen, Matt has asked her to phone him as soon as possible, and that was over half an hour ago. *Oh God, why didn't you check your phone, you idiot?* Wendy asks herself as she immediately clicks *call* next to Matt's name, before she checks any of his other messages.

"Wendy, are you okay?" Matt says urgently, answering his phone within a couple of rings to put Wendy to more shame.

"Yes, I'm fine, I'm still in the coffee shop. Emma has just left. I'm sorry, my phone was on silent for some reason. I'm really sorry. What's going on?"

"First, I'm okay, but we found Dad and he was still 'alive', but he has turned into some kind of undead zombie."

Matt pauses, expecting Wendy to ask a dozen questions, but she doesn't, she stays silent as if the news comes as no surprise to her. "Are you still there?" he asks.

"Yes, sorry Matt, I was just trying to process what you said. What happened?"

"We thought he was dead, but when the two police officers went to check him, Dad attacked them. I thought he was going to attack me too so I had to lock myself in his cage."

"Oh my God, Matt, I'm sorry; are you okay?" Wendy asks, shocked.

"Yes, I'm okay but I'm stuck in the cage. I don't know if you'll believe me, but after dad attacked them, they quickly turned into monsters too."

"Oh my God," Wendy says again, the blood draining from her face as her mind rushes to make sense of what Matt is telling her. "What's happening now, are they still there?"

"Well, shortly after, other people came to the house. I think they were police too and the two police officers dad attacked went upstairs and attacked them. I managed to keep Dad occupied with me, but I don't know what's happened upstairs. It has all gone quiet up there," Matt tells her quite calmly.

"You kept your dad with you?" Wendy questions.

"Yes, I wanted to stop him from attacking anyone else. I couldn't stop the other two though."

"And he is still in the basement?"

"Yes…" Matt starts, but a bleep interrupts him. "Bloody hell, my battery is about to go. I need you to listen, okay?"

"Yes Matt, go ahead."

"Can you go to the police station and tell them what is happening? If I phone them, they either won't believe me or they will send more officers, who will be attacked. You have to convince them of the danger and don't let them come unless they take precautions. Preferably tell them to send an armed unit."

"Okay," Wendy says.

"You don't sound very sure, Wendy. You have to tell them about the danger. If they just send normal police, Dad will attack them, do you understand?"

"Sorry, Matt. Yes, I understand. I was just trying to get it straight in my head, as it's a lot to take in."

"I know, I've been staring at a dad who's a zombie for a long time now, and I can't believe it myself. But it's real, I promise you."

"I believe you, Matt, of course. Are you going to be alright until the police get there?"

"Yes, he can't get in here."

"Okay, I'll be as quick as I can, just hold tight," Wendy tells him.

"I'm not going anywhere, just be as quick as you can Wendy."

"I will and I'll see you soon." Wendy hangs up.

Her mind racing, Wendy takes a breath for a second. When will her husband's madness end? How many more people's lives will be ruined by him, and when will she be free of his hold?

Those are questions for another time. Wendy quickly gets up from the table, her coffee untouched and she grabs her coat. She pushes her way through the busy coffee shop, not even noticing the waitress panicking that she is leaving without paying. Wendy swings the entrance door open and goes out into the cold dark evening to join the throngs of people, just as Emma had done. Only when she is outside and rushing away from the shop does she pull on her coat. The waitress comes out to stop her leaving, shouting as she does, but Wendy is quickly swallowed up into the crowds of shoppers and lost to the angry waitress.

The coffee shop is down a narrow side street just off Lemsfield's main square, where the main last-minute shopping rush is underway. The police station is on the other side of the square, so not too far, but with the crowds, it's not going to be a quick or easy walk for Wendy. She is having enough trouble leaving the narrow side street behind, what with the number of people bumbling around.

With a small amount of pushing and shoving, her fair share of uttering *excuse me* and apologising, Wendy arrives on the main square. At any other time, even with the large crowds, Wendy would pause for a moment and take in the intoxicating Christmas atmosphere that fills her local square. Christmas lights hanging from every available vantage point around the square, blaze in a multitude of festive colours. Strung overhead from one side to the other are thousands of tiny bright white twinkling lights that could easily fool you into thinking it is actually snow falling from the sky. Next to the tall Christmas tree, those who aren't panicking to find the last of their Christmas presents are gathered to watch the carol singers who fill the square with their seasonal vibes.

Wendy's only concern presently, however, is what the quickest route to the police station will be. She can't see the station from where she is, and that isn't because of the crowds. It is because the station is behind the church that fills up one side of the square. Having no choice but to go for it, Wendy tries to find a path between the people shopping and the crowds in the centre of the square, hoping she will find some breathing room in between the two.

Unfortunately, the breathing room is non-existent and every step that Wendy takes is a battle, no matter how many times she swerves to avoid shoppers who aren't looking where they are going. Of course, her urgency is lost on everyone, and they shuffle along at their own pace, weighed down with shopping bags and stopping whenever they spot something of interest, or just to look at their phones with no regard to anyone behind them. Wendy also has to wave away the street vendors trying to ply their wares to anyone and everyone, and who only add to the crush.

Wendy is quite frustrated and out of breath when she does finally make it to the other side of the square, but she has done it. She is so glad that she has worn a comfortable pair of her Converse trainers instead of the heels she nearly put on.

The old-fashioned blue police lantern that hangs on the wall above the street outside the police station is now within her sights, and Wendy fixes on it as she takes her turn at the corner of the square.

Arriving in front of the station, Wendy looks up the stairs that lead up to the entrance. Although she has walked past the steps many times before, she has never actually been into the police station, but then why would she have?

This should be interesting; she thinks as she starts to climb the steps. *How are you going to convince the police that the undead have risen in little old Lemsfield? They will think she has gone mad. You have to convince them*, she tells herself, *you have to for Matt. Don't take no for an answer and stick to your guns*. She climbs the steps with more conviction.

Wendy's hand reaches out for the long brass door handle as she gets to the top of the stairs but just as her hand goes to close around it, it's whisked away from her. The door of the police station is suddenly open and three burly male police officers rush out of the door, nearly knocking Wendy over. "Stand aside," one orders her as they go, and they don't look back to see if she is okay or to apologise for their rudeness.

Charming, Wendy thinks as she swiftly moves through the door before it closes behind the officers rushing away from the station, heading down the side of the church.

Inside, Wendy suddenly worries that the police officers' haste has something to do with what happened in the basement, with Matt? Wendy goes through the second set of doors and into the reception of the police station.

The reception desk is straight ahead of Wendy, in the spacious and ornate room in which she now finds herself. Fixed down the walls each side of the reception desk are cushioned benches for visitors to sit on while they wait, but Wendy goes directly to the desk.

Nobody is manning the desk, which is protected by a transparent Perspex shield. The chair behind is empty, and behind the chair is a dark grey wall with a door. She can't afford to wait and see if somebody is going to come and help her, as she needs to speak to an officer now. She quickly looks around for some way to call for assistance. She sees a button mounted on her side of the Perspex with a sign next to it reading, RING FOR ATTENTION. Wendy puts her finger on it and doesn't rush to release the button.

The button pressed, Wendy stands waiting in front of the desk, her patience wearing thin. After a couple of minutes, nobody has arrived to offer any assistance, and so Wendy presses the button again, this time leaving her finger on it for a longer amount of time. *This is an emergency*, she thinks, as her finger releases the button. *Surely that should send somebody out to at least see what the nature of the problem is?*

"Oh, this is ridiculous," Wendy mutters to herself after another couple of minutes have passed with still no sign of anyone coming out of the door at the back of the reception. She reaches for the button again. Just as she is about to press it, the door opens a quarter and a policewoman sticks her head through.

"Take a seat please, someone will be with you as soon as possible, Madam." And the policewoman's head starts to disappear back inside the doorway.

"This is an emergency!" Wendy protests. "I need to speak to someone immediately."

The policewoman's head pauses for a moment, just before it disappears, the policewoman looking directly at Wendy. "Take a seat, Madam, we have a major incident underway, so somebody will be out to see you as soon as possible." With that, the policewoman's head disappears and the door closes before Wendy can say another word.

How rude, Wendy thinks, but the words, 'major incident', strike fear into her. This has to be something to do with Matt. He said Armstrong and his partner were attacked and turned into zombies, and they then, by all accounts, went on to attack others who arrived at the house.

Wendy is at a loss as to what she should do. Should she press the button again and be more insistent, and not take no for an answer? Tell the policewoman that she knows what has happened? Surely, she would be interested in finding out what has caused this major incident, if they are indeed one and the same?

Wendy puts her finger back onto the button and leaves it there. Matt needs her help. She promised him she would convince the police, and that is exactly what she means to do.

Her finger begins to ache on the button as time passes, but she doesn't relent; she is determined to help Matt, one way or the other.

At least a few minutes pass, and just as Wendy is beginning to wonder if the buzzer is still sounding, wherever it does in the depths of the station, the door opens again. This time, an agitated policeman appears through the door. The three chevrons on his sleeve tell Wendy that he at least has some authority as a sergeant, and his older appearance suggests to her that he has experience too, which gives Wendy confidence that he can actually help her.

"Madam, please stop pressing the button. We have an emergency at the moment and as I believe my colleague told you, we will assist you as soon as we can. In the meantime, please..."

"I know what happened to Detective Armstrong," Wendy blurts out, cutting the sergeant off.

"What do you know of Armstrong?" the sergeant asks, surprised by Wendy's interruption and finally showing some interest.

"I know he was with my stepson when he and his partner were attacked, and my stepson is still in danger," Wendy informs him.

"One moment please," the sergeant says and quickly disappears back through the door.

"For God's sake," Wendy says out loud, her frustration getting the better of her as she looks up to the heavens, but only finds a CCTV camera looking down on her instead of an omniscient being.

To Wendy's relief, however, the door quickly opens again and two more police officers arrive behind the transparent shield. These two officers aren't in uniform. One is a rather haggard looking woman, who seems to have the weight of the world on her shoulders. The other is a worried-looking younger man, who Wendy would guess is her junior, or possibly her assistant.

"I have been informed that you know something of Detective Armstrong and Fleck," the woman says urgently.

"Yes, I do," Wendy starts and she goes on to tell the officers what she knows, together with what Matt has told her. The male officer stands to the side of the female and constantly takes down notes of Wendy's extraordinary story. Wendy is interrupted constantly by the woman, who asks Wendy probing questions or asks her to elaborate on sections of the information she is offering.

Paraphrasing as many elements of her statement as possible and leaving out any unimportant details, even with the interruptions, Wendy tells the officers what she knows in good time. She is more than a bit surprised that the officers don't discount anything she tells them out of hand, as far-fetched as some of it sounds, as it spills out of Wendy's mouth. They receive the information, more or less as a matter of fact, with growing looks of concern.

"Thank you, Mrs Bradley. Please take a seat while we process this information and decide on a course of action," Wendy is told by the junior officer when she finishes. They both turn to leave her in the lurch again.

"Hold on a minute!" Wendy insists. "My son needs help; what are you going to do about him?"

"I'm sorry, Mrs Bradley, whatever happened in your husband's basement isn't the only incident we are having to deal with. We have multiple reports of similar incidents, and every officer we have available has been despatched to deal with them. It sounds like your stepson is safe for the moment, and as soon as we have officers available, they will investigate your husband's house," the female officer tells Wendy.

"But..." Wendy tries to protest.

"Please be patient, Mrs Bradley, and take a seat. You'll be informed as soon as we have some information. I'm sorry, but that is the best we can do at the present time." With that, the two officers depart back through their door and Wendy is stranded again.

Disheartened and frustrated, Wendy does as she's told and ambles over to the uncomfortable looking bench on the left side of the room and slowly takes a seat. *What more could I have done?* she asks herself. More, she insists. I should have done more. Matt is relying on me?

Chapter 16

The carol singers have practised long and hard for their final performance of the festive season. The entire square erupts in applause when the last bars of their final carol builds to a euphoric crescendo that suddenly cuts off to leave the audience clapping and cheering ecstatically. Members of the choir clap along with the audience and exchange high fives between themselves, all smiling broadly in elation.

A raucous chant of, "We want more. We want more," quickly builds throughout the crowd, and the choir members look around at each other and to their conductor, all excited to give the crowd what they want. It is Christmas after all.

Above the chants, only the people on the very fringes of the audience hear the wailing screeches that echo off the buildings from the surrounding streets converging into the main square. But they take little notice of the inhuman noises, their focus quickly returning to the singers as they prepare for their encore.

A pretty young woman steps forward to the front of the stage, her nerves at leading off the encore plain for everyone to see. Her brightly knitted red and green Christmas jumper expands sharply as she fills her lungs with the air she will need to carry her first note. There isn't a hint of nerves in her angelic voice, however, as she raises her first note, one that carries on the crisp winter air to each corner of the square.

The entire audience hushes to silence when her mesmerising voice carries into their ears like an angel. They stare in wonder at the vision before them. They are sure she must have been sent down from heaven to sing to them.

So enchanted are the people in the audience with the young singer, that they don't notice the creature that has sprung onto the stage to join the choir.

The creature itself is transfixed by the glorious sound flowing out of the young woman for a moment, and it stalks towards her, pushing its way past the other members of the choir, who look at each other in confusion. More cheers rise from the crowd as the creature stumbles forward, the odd additional surprise to the show delighting them. Not even the choir's conductor takes exception to the intruder, his concentration focused entirely on his young protégé, whom he must direct to hold her note for as long as he deems fit.

Turning its ear towards the heavenly voice, the creature sniffs the air to savour the young woman's scent and then in a flash, and without ceremony, the creature pounces. A near-silence falls over the square as the angelic tones of the young woman's voice are rudely interrupted. The audience watches on excitedly as the two figures fall to the stage floor with a thud, their anticipation building as they wonder what direction the 'leftfield' show will take next.

Surely, Christmas is no time for Halloween costumes? Behind the two fallen figures, the choir gasps in shock. They all know that this isn't part of their arrangement, as does the conductor who looks on in confusion, his arms frozen in mid-air, and his anger building at the sudden invasion that has ruined his performance's rapturous finale.

Winded from her fall, the young singer blinks to focus on what, or who, has knocked her over, her breath returning. The face of the devil stares down at her, its hideous features distilling terror into her very core. She fights to release herself from the grip that pins her to the ground, to escape the evil eyes staring down at her.

She fills her lungs again, as she did moments before, to begin her performance. When her lungs release this time, however, an almighty ear-piercing scream washes over her audience, as the devil's face comes closer, its jaw extending open.

A confused hush remains over the square as the audience stare at the centre of the stage where the two figures roll around on the ground. The woman's scream is cut off as quickly as her song was, a sickly grunting noise rising to replace it. Audience members quietly begin to ask questions as the faces of the members of the choir change, and they back away from the figures.

Without warning, the head of the figure on top shoots up from where it was feasting down on the young woman. Now, the audience sees the beast for what it is, and the shock takes their breath away. The beast pushes itself upon its arms, above the still body below, to pronounce its horrific terror to the crowd. Deep red blood smeared around its lips and chin glistens in the twinkling lights and its mouth prises open again, to roar a deathly screech at its audience. A screech that doesn't go unanswered by the beast's brethren.

All at once, fear and panic take hold of the entire crowd. Screams break out spontaneously, shrilling into the night sky as parents grab their children off the ground and into their arms. People scatter to get away from the fearsome creature and the slaughter it promises, taking any avenue they can find a way from the stage.

The narrow streets and alleyways branching off the square cannot accommodate the sudden rush of people and become clogged, turning into bottlenecks. Shoppers, oblivious to the slaughter in their midst, push back against the sudden wave of people and hamper the evacuation still further. The unfortunate, who slip or don't possess the strength to fight to stay upright, fall to the ground to be trampled on by the hysterical crowd.

Back on the stage, the choir's time in the limelight has come to a terrifying end and they run for the stairs at the back of the stage. Each member is turning in fear at the gruesome creature behind them as they pile down the stairs, praying that the beast doesn't turn in their direction. It doesn't, as its hand claws at the body below, the beast looking out across the square at the swarms of prey running in every direction. The creature waits for its moment, until the hunt provides an easy picking for it to attack—and it doesn't have to wait long.

The creature sees the man run back towards the stage, its legs tensing up, its body edging forwards. Making a fatal decision, the man's arm reaches out for the large bag of shopping that he inadvertently left behind when he rushed his wife and children away from the front of the stage only moments before. His wife screams at him desperately from across the square, telling him to leave the bag; she doesn't care about the shopping, but his stupidity knows no bounds. The bag in hand, he lifts it like a trophy into the air, showing it off to his wife and smiling like a child who has just won a sports trophy at school.

The undead creature doesn't loiter. It jumps into action, pouncing down off the stage, and in a flash, it lands on its feet in the square, takes one more bounding step and launching itself at the unsuspecting show-off. It slams into the back of the man with such a force that he is catapulted forward off his feet, his wife's hysterical screams going unnoticed by her husband, or the creature.

Crashing into the ground face first, the crunching sound of breaking bone reverberates across the square as the shopping bag splits open, spilling its contents across the cobbled expanse. The creature loses its balance and topples forward too, but its fall has been broken by the man's body and it quickly scurries around to begin its next feed; the chilling screams it hears from across the square are of little consequence to it.

Seeing the creature jump down off the stage, the choir conductor turns away from the stairs that his colleagues are using and he rushes over to his fallen protégé who is lying at the front of the stage, where she is moving, if only in small fits.

Blood pools below the head and shoulders of his leading star, who has a voice the likes of which he has never heard in his many years of leading dozens of choirs. He quickly gets down on his knees next to her, desperate to see if there is anything he can do to help her, his face aghast at the horror that greets him. Tears well up in his eyes when he sees the gruesome hole that has been eaten away in her neck that contained her unique and beautiful vocal cords. Overcome with his remorse at the loss of such a beautiful voice and the promise it offered to his young protégée and to his career, his head drops down until it rests on her chest.

The body vibrates below his forehead, and even his sobs cannot disguise it. *What use is she to me now? She will never sing again, even if she does survive her horrific wounds*, the conductor thinks. His despair for his career deepens; it has taken so many years to find such a talent, many more years than the few he has ahead of him now.

Arms move around his shoulders and across his back. *Comforting arms,* he thinks to himself. His protégée must be feeling his sadness and despair, and even in her injured state, she wants to comfort him. The conductor suddenly comes back to his senses and goes to straighten his back, pushing against her arms, to witness the miraculous recovery for himself.

Her arms don't release their hold on him; however, they tighten around him, unyielding. Their vice-like grip pulls him down lower, his arms quickly moving to the stage floor to help resist their strengthening pull, but his efforts are futile.

The top of his head rolls forward, jammed against her breastbone, folding his neck inwards, and his chin squeezing tightly against his chest, making it almost impossible for him to breathe. He is powerless to stop the irresistible tightening of her grip, as the front of his neck crushes his windpipe in on itself.

He would cry out for help in his panic if he could, but it takes all of his efforts just to draw breath. A sharp pain cuts into the back of his extended neck, escalating his panic even further, his mind racing to figure out what is causing the shooting agony.

More excruciating pain arrives as he realises that it is his beloved protégée's teeth biting into him, that is the cause. The unforgiving teeth gnaw into his tender skin, ripping away his flesh until they tap against the bones of his spine. Even then, the teeth don't relent, but they continue to burrow into his spine's vertebrae and the soft matter contained between them.

The conductor's screams of agony and terror are only heard inside his fear-stricken head, his voice box crushed.

In an instant, the pain cuts off and his body goes completely limp, flopping down, as the evil teeth gnaw through his spinal cord, completely severing the nerve impulses between his body and his brain. The conductor's relief from his searing agony is almost worth the cost of the debilitating paralysis, but it doesn't relieve one ounce of his utter terror.

The unfolding, gruesome carnage and confusion send the general public into an uncontrolled frenzy, and chaos ensues. People stare out of the surrounding shops, wary to leave their sanctum as the hysteria outside escalates. Others run inside, fear etched onto their faces and shouting about zombies and slaughter. Inside the rammed bars, well-oiled patrons laugh off the impending doomsayers and order another round of drinks, refusing to let anything spoil their Christmas celebrations.

An infernal doom is falling over the small and ancient city centre of Lemsfield, and it threatens to overrun it. The bloodshed that has taken place in the square has sent the crowds scurrying into the adjoining streets and alleyways. Some are lucky and choose a route untainted by the infected beings and arrive back at their homes safely, or head into their cars to speed away from the danger area.

Those who choose the routes behind the church to escape, are moving into the territory of the undead. The unforgiving march of the undead into the city was initiated by the police officers who first came into contact with Bradley, in his basement.

Armstrong's tumble into the road from the side of the speeding police car has traumatised his body, but the injuries are insignificant compared to his need to feed. The paramedics had offered themselves up so readily and enthusiastically for him to quench his hunger, and he had gorged himself.

Jonathan Bradley's fatal infection has spread from there. Armstrong had willing accomplices to aid him spread the infection, in the form of two more police officers who transported Armstrong, disastrously straight into the busy shopping centre.

The unsuspecting public, relieved to have escaped the carnage of the square, now rush past the church and into the streets beyond, glad that they are safely on their way home. They mean to put the torrid scenes they have just witnessed behind them and carry on with the Christmas holidays as normal.

Strange and chilling screeching noises carry through the streets, however, carried on the breeze and bouncing off the tightly knit buildings. People look around urgently to see where the ominous noises are coming from, but they seem to emanate from nowhere and everywhere at the same time. Mothers and fathers pull their children along hastily. Some parents all but drag their youngsters along as their unease quickly grows.

Some parents with children small enough to carry pull them off the ground and into their arms, so that they can press ahead of the crowd, congratulating themselves for taking the initiative. They pull ahead, their arms and legs burning from the effort, which they are sure is a small price to pay for leaving the crowd behind and getting their loved ones to safety.

Ahead of them though, the shadows start to move disturbingly, and their confidence suddenly evaporates. The undead move out of the shadows, their horrifying and disfigured appearance coming into full focus under the themed street lighting, giving the overconfident leaders of the evacuating crowd the first glimpse of their fate.

Some people stand frozen in fear, while others turn and rush back to the crowd; there is safety in numbers, right? Perhaps some may manage to find refuge or miraculously slip past the undead, who now have the scent of the hunt, but many will not. They will be slaughtered beyond salvation, and the ones who do find salvation, will find themselves rising as a member of the undead.

Chapter 17

Wendy sits agitated, trying to get her behind comfortable and into a position where it doesn't feel as if it will slide off the bench at any moment and have her falling onto the dirt-ridden floor. She is convinced that if the bench were fitted inside the cells where the prisoners are held, they would consider their human rights violated and protests would be made; it is that uncomfortable. Obviously, whoever installed the bench decided to make it as uncomfortable as possible in the hopes that visitors to the police station would be put off staying for too long, and give up on the business they have with the police.

Wendy won't let herself be deterred so easily, Matt needs help and she means to make sure she gets it for him. She is, however, growing more and more concerned that the police have either forgotten about him or are just too busy for any officers to be available to help him. Nobody has come out of the door behind the shield to see if she is alright, never mind coming and updating her on the situation as she has been promised.

The room has remained deserted apart from her, but there has been plenty of activity in the foyer, next to the main entrance. Through the glass panels in the door, she has seen a constant stream of police officers rushing out of the main entrance from another part of the building.

Her concern growing, Wendy decides that she has been patient enough and gets up from the bench, her eye on the button she means to assault again. Before she can move, however, the reception door bursts open and a panicked man stumbles through it, closely followed by two young children and a woman. One of the children, a boy of no more than six years old, is in floods of tears and his older sister has a petrified look as if she might burst into tears at any moment too. The man rushes over to the reception counter and rams his finger on the button that Wendy was about to use. The mother follows the man over to the counter, pulling her children in close to her as she goes, shielding them as if they are in imminent danger.

Pressing the button brings the man no response, something Wendy knows all about, and she feels sympathy with his frustration. The panicked man is having none of it though, and raising his fist, he begins to hammer in on the Perspex. It booms under the barrage, filling the reception area with vibrating noise that sends the little girl into floods of tears, along with her brother. They both cower close, nestling into their mother who is on the verge of tears herself.

"What's happened?" Wendy says, stepping towards the mother, who looks at Wendy in fear as if she poses a threat to them.

"Th-th-there are monsters out there, killing people," the woman stutters in terror, and Wendy believes her immediately.

"Where are they?" Wendy asks deadly seriously, almost having to shout over the booming noise.

"In the square, on the stage, the singer was slaughtered, and another man."

Wendy's stomach drops, a feeling of dread taking hold of her. Her mind races at the woman's words; how could they be in the square that she has only recently walked through? They must have come from Bradley's basement, she is sure of that; but how did they get into the square?

"How many are there?" Wendy asks, but before the woman can answer, the main door of the reception flies open again and more terrified people rush into the room.

"Mike," the woman shouts to her husband as the people pour in, and Wendy watches as he leaves the counter to move in front of his family, herding them back towards the counter.

Another man pushes past everyone and takes up Mike's position at the counter; he too presses the button and then starts banging on the Perspex. Suddenly, the room is filling up quickly as more people pile in, all displaying panicked looks.

"It's not safe here, Mike," the woman insists to her husband, but he has a vacant look, not knowing what to do for the best.

Wendy looks up to the CCTV camera hovering above them all. She knows that the people behind the grey door must be watching the commotion in the reception area, but still, nobody comes out of it to offer any assistance. Or is Wendy wrong, and have all the police left the building and the camera has no audience? There have been enough officers piling out of the building, so are they all on the streets, trying to restore order? Wendy doubts that, as she has to move farther over to the side as the room keeps filling up. They wouldn't leave the station unmanned and must realise that the reception is full of people; the sheer noise would tell them that even if nobody is watching through the camera.

A horrible feeling of guilt is building in Wendy as she looks around at the terrified faces packed into the police station's reception. It is her husband who is the cause of this horror, which is spreading at an extraordinary rate… and it was she who bit into him, so that makes her responsible too. Adding to her guilt is the knowledge that she could have put a stop to this weeks ago if she had just told the police the truth in the first place, and hadn't withheld her information because, 'she wasn't feeling up to it'. *You selfish fucking bitch; look what you have brought onto these people*, she tells herself, *look what you are responsible for!*

Stop feeling sorry for yourself, what are you going to do about it? Wendy asks herself angrily.

"Come on, let's get outta here," Mike says to his wife. "They obviously aren't coming."

"Where we going to go?" his wife asks worriedly.

"We will have to try and get back to the car."

"I'm not sure, Mike," the woman says, looking down at her children with concern.

"It's not safe here, you said it yourself. Anything could come through that door, or one of these people could change. We don't know," Mike reasons.

"I know, but going outside, you saw what those things did."

"What other option have we got? Come on, it isn't that far to the car." And with that, Mike begins to barge him and his family toward the exit door.

Wendy listens with chills running through her as she wonders what the 'things' the woman mentioned are like. She nearly asks the couple that question, so that she knows for sure, but that would just be selfish of her; they have their own problems.

The reception area has become jam-packed with people in varying stages of hysteria, and the pressure of the room is only adding to the growing feeling of anger she has towards her lunatic of a husband. Wendy knows exactly where the monster is, but has she got the guts to end the fucker herself and save Matt at the same time?

Wendy turns to follow the family out of the police station as they create a hole through the rammed reception. She isn't sure if she has got the guts to face Bradley by herself, but she is determined to try, if only for Matt and no one else.

Wendy pushes through the crowded people toward the exit, looking at the shock on their faces as she goes. Whatever they have witnessed was horrifying, that is plain to see. Well, *I have faced down the beast once and I will do it again, but this time for good*, she tells herself.

Eventually, and with considerable effort, especially with the small children, the family manage to push their way through the reception and out into the foyer, Wendy following them every step of the way.

The main door is jammed open and Wendy can see that the family are, at least, relieved to feel the fresh air in their lungs again, as she is. The family stop at the top of the small stairway to get their bearings, before they continue on to find their car.

Surprise and dread hit Wendy as she looks out of the station at the square to her right, and the street in front of her. The landscape has changed considerably in the short time since she entered the police station in the hopes of finding help. Only discarded litter covering the ground remains of the crowds that filled the square and lined the streets.

There are people still around, scurrying this way and that, or making a break for it out of the shops. But the majority of the crowd has evaporated into the outskirts of the city, leaving the centre deserted and ghostly in comparison to how it was only a short time ago.

An ominous screech echoes across the city, sending fear into Wendy's stomach. She has heard that horrific sound before, in Bradley's basement. The family next to her look at each other petrified as they hear the noise, the children clinging on to the closest parent, their confidence in finding their car waning.

"Where are you parked?" Wendy asks the family.

"In the church hall car park," Mike tells her nervously.

"I am going that way. I know the area well, as I live here. I can show you if you like?"

Mike and his wife look at each other for a second before nodding and accepting Wendy's offer, obviously grateful for the company.

"Okay, good," Wendy says. "Just give me one second."

Wendy pulls the small handbag she has brought with her off her shoulder, and quickly opens it. She takes her phone out and without looking at it, stuffs it in her front jeans pocket and takes her wallet out to put in her back pocket. Her keys go into her padded jacket that she zips up, and she then throws the bag onto the floor. There is nothing else she needs in it and she has a feeling it might just get in the way.

"I'm Wendy, by the way," she says.

"I'm April," the woman tells Wendy. "This is Mike and down here, we have Sarah and Peter."

"Nice to meet you all, are you ready?" Mike and April nod to confirm they are, and Wendy's foot reaches for the first step down.

As she descends, Wendy feels a sickening tightness in her belly and has visions of a soldier going into battle. *Is this how it feels*, she wonders, *to go to war*? If it is, she wishes she had a weapon to accompany this awful feeling.

Going left and away from the square, Wendy leads the family down the street adjacent to the church. Their car park, unfortunately, is completely on the other side of it. They are going to have to make their way around the shops at the back of the church to get to it, since there is no cut through to shorten the distance.

Wendy doesn't hang around, and she moves quickly down the street, the church on their right and shops on their left as they leave the station behind. Her eyes are scanning everywhere in front of them, looking into the lights of shop entrances and the shadows around the church, constantly checking for anything that might be lurking.

Footsteps run upon them from behind threateningly, and Wendy spins around in terror to confront them, along with April and Mike. Wendy's fists are raised ready to fight, as if she were a boxer, despite the fact she has never punched anyone or anything in her life. *There's a first time for everything*, Wendy tells herself as she prepares for confrontation.

Relief washes over them all, as a policeman runs up the street at them, his hi-vis jacket swaying side to side as his chunky black boots hit the ground.

"Officer," April pleads as the man draws level with them, but he doesn't stop. He doesn't even acknowledge her as he runs past them. "For fuck's sake, charming that is," April moans as the back of his hi-vis jacket disappears into the distance.

"Come on, let's keep moving," Wendy encourages as she sets off again, stalking ahead.

After the church, more shops lead down to a brightly lit intersection that has an illuminated Christmas star hanging over the centre of it. Wendy approaches the intersection cautiously, Mike by her side and the rest of the family slightly behind. Other people cross the walkways, heading in different directions, some moving quickly whilst others go slow, like Wendy and the family. As they get closer, horrible sounds become louder, sounds of screaming and death, that seem to be coming from every direction ahead.

"Dad," Sarah's scared little voice says as she holds her mother's hand, looking for reassurance.

"It's okay, the car isn't far now," Mike tells her, trying to sound confident, but knowing it's actually still some way off.

Mike looks at Wendy for reassurance himself and she attempts a smile, but Mike's face tells her it wasn't a smile she managed; it was a grimace. She turns away from him, looking ahead as they arrive at the intersection where they need to turn right, but she is nervous to move out into the open and expose them all.

"Is there no other way?" April asks.

"Afraid not. Only back through the square and around the other side of the church," Wendy replies.

"Come on, we might as well get on with it," Mike says as he starts to move.

Mike takes the lead and edges them around the corner of the intersection, but Wendy grabs his arm to stop him as she suddenly sees a strange, limping figure emerging from the shadows of the street ahead. Somehow, Wendy knows that the figure isn't human, whether by the way it is moving or something else.

"Get behind me, into that doorway," Wendy tells April and the children. She has no idea why she said it or what she hopes to do to stop this creature if it takes an interest in them. The words just come out.

Behind her, Wendy hears the children snivelling in fear as she helps shepherd them into the alcove of the closest dark doorway. Her concentration is fixed ahead though, as she and Mike use their bodies to block the doorway.

She can't take her eyes off the sinister figure about to cross into the light of the intersection. There is no doubt in her mind that it is one of the undead stalking closer, and they can only hope that its attention will be diverted elsewhere before it sees them. Wendy finds herself hoping and praying that someone else will use the intersection to divert the creature, even though she knows what the terrible consequences would be for the poor soul.

Nobody uses the intersection, so there is no opportunity for them to escape and the creature keeps coming, and passes under the lights of the Christmas star, heading straight for them. Beside her, Wendy hears Mike breathing heavily as he sees the grotesque creature in the light for the first time, its hideous features plain to see and the features fixed upon them.

Perhaps it is her feeling of guilt that drives Wendy to do what she does next, or maybe, she just cannot bear the thought of this young family being ripped apart by the beast. Whatever the reason and with little thought for herself, Wendy steps out of the darkness and protection the alcove offers, and stands between the creature and the family.

She doesn't want to die and certainly doesn't want to become one of the undead. Her heart races as terror suddenly takes hold of her, the realisation of the danger in which she has put herself sinks in. Nevertheless, she stands her ground as the beast comes towards her, its dead eyes staring and its mouth beginning to part. Again she raises her fists, as if they will offer her any protection from such a ferocious animal.

The creature, unsurprisingly, is unconcerned by Wendy's feeble display of defiance and it comes straight for her, its grizzly teeth on show. “Get the fuck away!” Wendy yells at the beast as ferociously as she can, and to her amazement, the creature pauses. She stares at the creature, straight into its evil eyes, showing it that she isn't afraid of it, despite terror threatening to overwhelm her completely.

Wendy's game of blink with the monster doesn't last for long, and the creature snarls at her and steps closer. *This is it*, Wendy thinks, and panics as the beast reaches out ready to take her. *There is no escape, not this time! This is the end.* Visions of the basement and the torment Bradley put her through flash through her mind, and she feels anger growing inside her.

She sees Matt too, trapped in Bradley's cage. She promised to help him and save him; how can she let him down when he needs her, and he is relying on her help?

Her rage spirals out of control at the creature threatening to stop her, and she lunges at it, a snarling noise escaping her mouth. Wendy's rage is uncontrollable, a terrifying rage that she has only felt once before, in Bradley's basement, at the end when his powerful hands tightened around her throat. Wendy sees the beast's face change instantly, like a wild animal that has met its match and it cowers a little, its arms dropping.

A fierce growl rises from deep within Wendy, and she directs it straight at the beast, her throat vibrating from the force, her behaviour unexplainable.

Suddenly, the creature looks unsure of its course of action and glances away from Wendy's staring eyes. It looks down the street from where Wendy and the family have just come. *Is it looking for easier pickings?* Wendy wonders, and she snarls at it again, to force the issue.

Behind Wendy, Mike looks on in astonishment, as does April as she clings onto her children tightly, hiding their faces from the horrific creature. They stand and bear witness as this unassuming woman they have just met faces down the undead creature. The woman doesn't relent until the creature turns and moves away from them, and they watch on in amazement as it walks quickly away, towards the police station.

"Are you okay?" Mike asks nervously.

"Yes, I'm fine," Wendy replies, her voice rasping. She quickly tries to calm herself; she doesn't want to frighten the family and daren't turn to look at them for fear her face might do just that. She has no idea what her face looks like, but something tells her the rage has contorted her appearance.

Gradually, Wendy feels her heartbeat slow and the rage diminish, and she risks turning to face Mike and April. Both have looks of astonishment and she sees a flash of fear cross their face as they look at her, but neither says a word.

"Let's get moving," Wendy says, her voice more her own now.

"How did you do that?" Mike asks.

"It's a long story and we haven't the time; we need to get you to your car."

Mike doesn't argue or press the issue. "Lead the way," he tells Wendy, glancing at April as he does. Wendy suspects that even though they don't know how Wendy faced down the creature, they are both suddenly very pleased to have her with them.

Wendy's confusion at her behaviour probably amounts to more than theirs combined. She thought that the overpowering rage that took hold of her when she bit into Bradley was a one-off, but now it has surfaced again. She had assumed that her illness, that the chemicals she had been subjected to and that were in her system, had caused her behaviour. Was she wrong, and has Bradley's treatment changed her for good? Is the rage part of her now, and could it resurface at any time?

God, so many questions, Wendy thinks as she carefully leads them around the corner and onto the street that leads to the car park. *This is not the time to be questioning yourself*, she tells herself, *your concentration needs to be on getting this family safely to their car, and then it needs to be on Matt.*

Ahead of them as they turn the corner, Christmas lights span from one row of shops to the other on the opposite side. The small multistorey car park they are aiming for is visible at the end of the shops in relative darkness, compared to the brightly lit approach.

"I can't believe how quiet it is already," Mike observes from just behind Wendy.

"I know. At the first sign of zombies on the street, everyone is running for the hills," Wendy jokes, but nobody laughs. "Sorry, ignore me, that was in poor taste. It's my nerves," Wendy says, disappointed in herself for even attempting the joke.

"Don't worry, you're not the only one who is nervous," April reassures her.

"Get back!" Wendy suddenly warns quietly, the joke instantly forgotten.

Immediately, Mike and April do as Wendy says and dart into another doorway with their children as figures appear, scurrying from the front of one of the shops close by.

Relief washes over them all quickly, however, as they see it is only a group of people making a break for it. The group, who don't notice them, move in quick time in the same direction as they are heading, their heads ducked down as they run.

"Come on," Wendy says urgently, deciding to follow the group, who could well be heading for the car park.

"Oh, my God," April whispers from behind Wendy, before she has a chance to move. The terror in her voice is obvious and Wendy turns to see what has frightened her so much.

Wendy's stomach drops as she follows April's gaze back to the intersection they have just left behind. The undead are filing out into the intersection, their twisted appearance unmistakable, as is the direction they are heading in. The creatures are coming straight for them.

"Move it," Wendy orders, cursing the group ahead, whose sudden arrival out in the open, she is sure, has attracted the creatures to head in their direction.

A deathly screech reverberates off the building's frontages around them, bouncing into their ears. The children whimper in fear as their mother and father drag them from their paltry refuge in the doorway and pull them out into the open. Their parents know that they have only one option, and that is to make a run for it. Only death, or worse, waits for them if they remain in the doorway.

April whisks Peter into her arms within a few steps, his legs too small to outrun the undead zombie horde and Mike quickly follows her lead by whisking Peter's elder sister up. And the children's parents run as they have never run before, despite the heavy loads weighing them down. Their fear for their offspring drives them on, no matter how much their bodies protest.

Wendy runs beside them, unable to help carry their load. All she can do is escort the family as they run for their lives, willing them on and praying that they make it to safety. But safety is no more than futile wishful thinking right now. Wendy knows it; the car park is still a distance away and the horde is closer and faster, they will never make it to the car park in time.

Should they dive into one of the open shop doorways, the one the other group has just emerged from? What would that gain them? Nothing. The undead would surely follow them inside and they would be trapped, with no escape.

"Keep running… faster," Wendy screams from beside the family.

Their only option is to keep going and to at least try and outrun their murderous pursuers, no matter how long the odds. Ahead, Wendy sees that the group have seen the threat careering through the streets and coming up quickly behind them. They have all lifted their legs and gone into full sprints too, and they are stretching farther in front, close to the car park.

Panic grips Wendy as she feels the creatures gaining on them, but she daren't look back over her shoulder. Her eyes stay fixed ahead, hoping for salvation, and then suddenly, there is a glimmer of hope.

Upfront, a man at the rear of the group looks back over his shoulder, and Wendy sees his wide, petrified eyes and for a split second, they look at her. That second is fatal, his legs lose track of their direction and his right foot clips the back of his left heel as it runs forward. His balance is lost, and the man flies forward with nothing to stop his trajectory but the concrete slabs on the ground in front of him. His arms shoot out in reflex to protect him from his fall, but his speed is too great for them to handle and he smashes into the ground. The thud of his skull crashing onto the concrete is sickening, and his legs fly up into the air behind him until his spine cannot bend anymore and they fall back down onto the ground.

The man still hasn't moved an inch when Wendy and the family chase past his stationary body and none afford him a look as they pass. They can only hope that he is unconscious, for his sake, if the undead horde does decide to pay him attention. They hear its pursuit fade momentarily as they pile into the body.

Taking the gamble, Wendy glances back for just a second to see if their pursuers have all been diverted by the fresh meat they have been offered. Her heart sinks when she sees that only a few have taken the bait and there are at least five or six still on their tails.

The creatures have fallen back though, if only a little, the pack's leaders having accepted the fallen prey. But Wendy's speed is slowing as April flags at her side. Peter is weighing her down, her exhaustion eating away at her stamina, and it is only a matter of time before they are swallowed up, into the horde.

Looking desperately ahead, the car park is close and yet still so far, but the group in front has suddenly disappeared. Have they succeeded in making it to the car park or taken another route to safety?

The light suddenly fades, and Wendy nearly stumbles down the kerb that drops her onto the road, as they leave the shops and the Christmas illuminations behind. Shadows follow them down onto the road, the creature's arms reaching out towards April's back, so close now.

"Run, April," Wendy shouts hysterically as the creature threatens to pull April down with Peter. And April does. She gives it all that she's got.

The concrete car park looms over them so closely that Wendy can see the entrance the cars drive into with the pedestrian door positioned next to it. She discounts the door immediately. There is no way they will have time to slow to open it, so they must use the entrance reserved for cars. April is flagging again though, and there's no way they will even make it that far, since the stamina of the creature behind them seems unbreakable.

Wendy looks urgently for an alternative, anything that might offer them salvation. The other group can't have disappeared into thin air; they must be somewhere?

Car headlights flash across Wendy's vision, almost out of nowhere, and it takes her a second to figure out the car has just sped out of the car park. *That's where they disappeared to*, Wendy thinks, as the car tyres screech on the road's surface. But the car is pointed in the wrong direction to drive out of the city centre. Its headlights are pointing at them and they are approaching at speed.

"Faster," Wendy shouts as she realises what the driver of the car is planning as it swerves around the very edge of the road. Wendy sees the car packed with people as it speeds past her to swerve again, its headlights shining onto the creatures pursuing, as it piles into them.

Grim sounds of thudding and breaking bones fill Wendy's head as the car crashes into the creatures, taking at least four or five of the beasts out in one fell swoop. The noises are accompanied by hideous squeals of suffering as the car drives through and over the bodies, one of which is thrown up onto the car's bonnet to be ejected up and over the back of the speeding hunk of metal.

Terrible noises they may be, but they bring a small amount of relief to Wendy when she sees the creatures fall and get driven over, the car bouncing as its wheels crush them into the tarmac. Wendy's relief is short-lived, however, as one creature is out of the car's reach and is still on its feet, the one directly behind April, whose stamina has left her completely.

Mike sees it too and stops instantly, releasing Sarah from his arms to drop down onto her feet before he dives to the side. Peter flies from his mother's arms as she is dragged down by the creature that grabs onto her back. April's terrified scream resonates through the air as she feels the beast grab her and she is forced to release Peter to crash into the road.

April watches her son shoot forward through the air, her concern only for him as her arms flail out to try and break her own fall. Her scream suddenly cuts off as she sees her husband catch and save Peter, inches from the solid surface he is about to crash into, moments before she hits the ground herself.

Wendy grinds to a halt and watches in horror as the horrific creature grabs it prey and drags April, smashing into the roadside. Mike rolls away with Peter in his arms as the beast closes in on the back of April, its eyes fixed on the exposed flesh on the back of her neck.

April is not moving when Wendy's legs push her forward with as much force as they can muster, straight at the creature primed to feast on April. Wendy's shoulder slams into the side of the beast and her head collides into the beast's skull with such a force it knocks stars into her eyes.

Dazed, Wendy finds herself on her back in the middle of the road, looking up at the stars above that are interlacing with the ones caused by her head's collision. The sound of screeching tyres is distant as the ominous shadow rises next to her from the road. She barely registers the car zooming past her but when it's gone, so too is the ominous shadow.

“April,” Wendy hears Mike shout, as she manages to push herself up into a sitting position, her head still spinning. Her neck protests in pain as she turns to see Mike crouched over his wife, their two children standing behind them, looking down in shock at their mother's forlorn body.

“I'm okay,” April suddenly mutters as she starts to push herself up and off the road.

“Wendy saved you from the monster,” Sarah says as a matter of fact, and she runs around her mother to help Wendy as she tries to get to her feet as her head begins to clear.

“Thank you, Sarah,” Wendy says as she stands and looks at the scene around her. Mike is helping April up off the road as Peter clings to his own hurt leg. Her hands are grazed, bleeding and filled with pieces of tarmac but thankfully, that seems to be the worst of her injuries.

The car, that like a superhero came to their rescue and then disappeared, has driven off without a by-your-leave, but it has left a trail of undead carnage in its wake.

Twisted bodies litter the road all around them, the zombies in various states of disfigured and gruesome distress and yet, alarmingly, the corpses still move. None, however, poses an immediate threat due to their catastrophic injuries, but Wendy wouldn't like to stray too close to them. Something tells her they would still bite if they had the chance, no matter how shattered their bones are or how much their wounds ooze.

“We need to move,” Wendy instructs Mike and April urgently. The sound of death is close, and not just from the undead at their feet.

Something touches Wendy's hand and she looks down to see Sarah looking up at her. Wendy smiles at the little girl and takes her hand in hers before she follows Mike towards the car park. April is limping, but Mike helps her and in no time, they reach the entry to the car park.

"What level are you on?" Wendy asks before they go in.

"We're on the first."

"Okay, let's use that door. The stairs aren't as exposed as walking through parked cars," Wendy says, pointing at the pedestrian door.

Mike moves to the door without question, and they are soon climbing up the well-lit stairs to the first floor. April finds it tough going up the stairs with her painful leg, but she manages it and they find themselves at the door to the first level.

"Hold your mum's hand, Sarah, while I check to see if the coast is clear," Wendy says, releasing Sarah's hand.

The blue-painted door is solid with no glass panel to peer through, so Wendy carefully opens it up slightly so that she can get a look through into the car park beyond. Thankfully, the car park itself is also well-lit and Wendy doesn't see anything untoward and hears nothing but the strange sound a quiet car park seems to make, as sounds from the outside filter into it and the strip lights buzz. She pulls the door open fully so that Mike and April can squeeze through with their children, and she then follows them as they make their way to the car.

About half of the car park spaces are vacant and Wendy wonders where the owners of the remaining cars are? It's only a relatively small car park but there are still plenty of spaces still occupied.

Mike's car is close to the entrance and his lights flash as he quickly presses the button to open it. Wendy waits, thinking while Mike takes April around to the passenger side and eases her into her seat before he rushes to get his children inside also.

"Where can we drop you, Wendy?" Mike says when his family is safely inside the car.

"Thank you, Mike, but I'm going to leave you here," Wendy replies.

"No way, I'm not abandoning you here, Wendy."

"You don't have a choice. Get your family to safety. Where do you live?"

"We live in Sutton, so not far, and we will drop you wherever you want. We owe you that much."

"Thanks, Mike, but you don't owe me anything," Wendy says, her guilt for her hand in this nightmare coming back to haunt her. "I've got some important business to take care of just up the road and don't want to put your lovely family in any more danger, so please go straight home."

"I will never forgive myself if I leave you here like this, and neither will April, or the children for that matter," Mike pleads.

"I will speak to April, but my son is close and he needs my help," Wendy says, and walks away from Mike to go around to the passenger side.

April protests and becomes emotional when Wendy says her goodbyes, as do the children. Wendy promises that they will meet up once this 'horrible episode' is over, and swaps numbers with April, but then insists that she has to leave them.

Wendy has a tear in her eye by the time she closes the back door after Sarah demands to give Wendy a goodbye hug, in which Peter joins. Mike is still standing at the back of the car waiting for her when she has finished, with a solemn look on his face.

"Please get in the car," he begs.

"I can't, but I do need to ask a favour."

"Of course, anything, name it."

“Have you got any tools in the car, or something heavy, please?” Wendy asks.

“What like a weapon?” Mike asks, confused—but knows the answer before she replies.

“Exactly,” Wendy says.

“I don’t think this is a good idea, Wendy.”

“Please, Mike, have you?”

Mike presses another button on his key fob and his boot magically opens slowly. He leans in and pulls up the bottom floor to reveal the compartment containing the car’s spare wheel and associated tools.

“This is the only tool there is that could be used as a weapon,” Mike says, holding up a tyre iron.

“That’s good enough, just in case,” Wendy replies, taking the heavy steel tool off him.

She holds it, weighing it by the handle that has a pointy bit at the end, and she looks up its length to where it bends at ninety degrees, by the socket on the end that fits the wheel nuts. “I’ll get it back to you,” Wendy tells him.

“Don’t worry about that, just make sure you get back safely,” Mike replies sincerely.

“I plan to, now get your family out of here, Mike.”

Mike surprises her by taking a step forward and reaching over to hug her around her shoulders. “Thanks for your help and please be careful,” he tells her.

“I will, goodbye,” Wendy says and turns to leave before she changes her mind and leaves with her new friends.

“Goodbye, Wendy. Let us know when you're safe,”

“You too,” Wendy replies as she walks away without looking back.

Chapter 18

The tyre iron begins to weigh heavily in Wendy's hand before she has even made it to the bottom of the stairs, and back onto the ground floor. The ache the weight brings to her hand reminds her that she isn't infallible and she begins to wonder if perhaps she should have got into the car when Mike insisted. She could have got to safety and then decided on the best course of action to help Matt. As the police said, he isn't in immediate danger.

She hears a car's engine as it drives through the car park and she waits in the bottom alcove of the stairwell for a moment, until she hears the car speed away, before she reaches for the door handle. Her hand closes around the cold metal of the handle but it pauses there as her thoughts get caught up in the task ahead and the dangers she is about to walk into.

Bradley's house is probably a six or seven-minute walk from where she is. It would be less if she cut through the park, but she really doesn't fancy walking through the exposed dark areas of the park, not with the undead on the prowl. Much better to stay on the streets, she decides, and her hand tightens on the handle, but then releases it.

Matt, she thinks, *tell him you're coming,* and she retrieves her phone from her pocket with her free hand. The voicemail symbol is displayed when she opens her phone, and she eagerly swipes to check who it is from. But it isn't Matt who has tried to get hold of her, it is Emma.

Emma will have to wait a moment, Wendy thinks, *Matt is more urgent right now.* And she retrieves his number and presses call. After a moment's silence, her phone connects straight to his voicemail. *'Shit,'* she says to herself, *Matt did say his battery was on its way out, so it must have given up the ghost.* She doesn't leave a message. She plans to see him before he will have a chance to charge his phone again. Instead, she connects to her voicemail to see what Emma has to say. Again, she is left frustrated and greeted with silence. Emma leaves no message, which worries Wendy and so she is forced to call her back.

"Hi Wendy," Emma says after answering quickly.

"Are you alright?" Wendy asks hastily.

"Yes, I'm fine. I came straight home. I couldn't face the shopping, but I'm feeling a bit better now so I'm going to pop back to do it shortly with Mum and Dad. Hopefully, it will have quietened down too. Are you home?"

"Don't come into the town. It's not safe. Stay home, Emma!" Wendy says sharply.

"What d'you mean?"

Wendy has to think for a second, not sure what to tell Emma. "The infection, the one that Bradley and I had, it's spreading. I know it sounds farfetched but it's turning people into zombies that are killing people; it's chaos here, so promise me you'll stay at home, Emma," Wendy says desperately.

"Zombies?" Emma says doubtfully.

"Yes, Emma, I can't explain anymore. I've got to go to Matt. Turn on the news, I'm sure something will come on about it, if it's not already. Promise me you'll stay home."

"Yes, Wendy, I promise. Where are you?" Emma questions.

"Don't worry about me. I'll phone you again later, okay? Now I've got to go."

"Okay, phone me later, though, won't you?" Emma says with confusion in her voice.

"I will, but stay in tonight, okay? Speak later," Wendy finishes, and hangs up.

She is sure Emma will stay at home, even if she thinks that Wendy has gone stark raving mad. It is lucky they spoke. Emma and her parents could have been making their way into this nightmare if they hadn't. Hopefully, she will switch on the news and see for herself. There must be some coverage of it on there by now, surely?

Wendy rams her phone back into her pocket, switches hands with the tyre iron, and then pulls the car park door open with new vigour to get this finished.

Far from rushing out of the door, however, Wendy checks the lie of the land before she makes any move to go outside. She has come too far to run blindly out into the cruel night, and the sounds of death in the air reaffirm her need to be cautious.

Despite the hideous echoes of suffering, the night seems strangely still. A typical cold December evening has enveloped the city. The night sky is crystal clear and pitch black, save for the countless shining stars. The moon is nowhere to be seen, to illuminate the twisted bodies that the car mutilated, away to the left of the car park. The bodies have gone quiet, which gives Wendy some solace as she steps out of her refuge, although she is sure the undead corpses are only waiting for the whiff of human meat to stir them up again.

Across from the car park and adjacent to the shopping centre is a small row of dark and uninviting office blocks that have been abandoned for the Christmas holidays.

Wendy doesn't want to go back through the shopping centre, or through the park, so her route is set and will take her along the Church Road between the offices and the park. The road is old and narrow with offices and apartments on one side that overlook the park on the other. Wendy is hoping that it will offer little to attract the undead, and so not pose a threat.

We will see, Wendy thinks as she walks into the road, her eyes darting in every direction. The tragic screaming is definitely coming from her left, back towards the shopping centre and the square, Wendy thinks as she crosses the road.

She turns in the opposite direction to join Church Road, and as she walks around onto it, she takes it nice and steadily, searching for any sign of the undead.

Church Road is quiet, thankfully, the office buildings dark, but the apartments are lit up brightly with Christmas lights and decorations in the windows. Silhouettes stand peering out of the many windows like ghouls, looking down on the road below in trepidation. The dark heads of the silhouettes dart down in Wendy's direction as she walks along, fearful of Wendy's presence, and who can blame them? Their quaint, picturesque city has inexplicably become the epicentre of the apocalypse. They must be petrified, and it's happened right on the cusp of Christmas, to boot. Wendy also suddenly realises that perhaps the people are searching for friends and loved ones who were out tonight enjoying the festivities, but have yet to return home.

Swapping hands with the tyre iron once again, Wendy makes quick progress along Church Road, grateful that it is clear. This is the calm before the storm, she knows that, because at the end of Church Road, she is going to have to turn left, back towards the mayhem to reach her destination. There is no way around that, unless she takes a long diversion, and the thought of Matt trapped in the basement with Bradley won't allow her to do it.

A small child waves methodically at Wendy from the window of one of the lower apartments near the end of Church Road. The child's vacant eyes follow Wendy from the shadows as it waves at her, as if the child were sending Wendy off to war. Perhaps the child knows more than Wendy does? Whatever the reason, the haunting child gives her an ominous feeling as she is about to reach the end of the road and head back in the direction of the undead chaos.

Not responding to the chilling child and trying to ignore it, doesn't stop the unwanted feeling of dread rising within her, and Wendy is glad when the window is firmly behind her.

That's the first part of the journey over, Wendy thinks as she reaches the end of Church Road that now bends around to the left. *The easy part is done at least*, she tells herself.

She must now make her way along a residential street that has numerous adjoining roads, and all that are on the left side run into the city centre, the shops and the danger area. The houses on the right-hand side have the park at the back.

The road that she plans to take is off to the right and away from the centre, which is a fair distance along. Once she is able to turn onto that road, Wendy is hoping that the side streets that will lead to Bradley's house will be as quiet as Church Road, although absolutely nothing is guaranteed.

The hard steel gripped in Wendy's right hand is the only small bit of reassurance she has when she edges around the corner. Sounds of violence and carnage greet Wendy for the next part of her journey and in the near distance, she can see the cause of the harrowing noises.

Ahead, moving in the night are the unmistakable figures of the undead. They stumble about aimlessly through the shadows before wandering through the spotlights of the streetlamps above, that shine down to highlight their fearsome appearance. *There are so many of them*, Wendy shivers, knowing there is no other way to go, but determined to proceed.

She keeps low and rushes across the two-lane road. The parked cars lining it will at least afford her some cover, she reasons, as she reaches the other side. She peers down the pavement between the cars and the houses and sees that nothing moves.

The creatures are all on the other side of the road, where the interconnecting streets into the centre are. She presumes that is where they have been picking off the unfortunate souls as they try to escape the city centre and she can only hope they stay there, at least until she passes.

Treading carefully and staying down behind the cover of the cars, she makes her way closer to the hungry horde. The houses opposite the cars are all dark and spooky, none of the residents daring to switch on even the dimmest of lights, for fear it would attract death to their door. Doors, that open straight out onto the street, don't even have front gardens to offer a barrier against the threat, or an escape route for Wendy if she needs one.

The closer Wendy gets to the road she needs to use, the more she moves into harm's way. Retching and screeching noises become louder and louder as she moves behind the cars parked adjacent to the horde, and the sound bounces off the houses to torment her. Her legs ache terribly from using the muscles she never normally does use as she shuffles along, crouched and with legs bent, behind the cars, which luckily are tightly parked together to conceal her.

Wendy makes good progress and quickly nears the junction of the road, and only then does she realise that she has a problem. Double yellow lines painted onto the roadside have left a long section before the junction with no parked cars to hide her. *Shit*, she thinks as she rests her back onto one of the last parked cars before the junction, to debate her next move.

Her vision wanders over to the house opposite while her brain works, and something catches her attention. At the bottom of the dark ground floor window, a haunting pair of wide-open eyes appear, as the top of somebody's head appears behind the glass. The apparition startles Wendy initially, but it quickly becomes apparent to her that the owner of the saucer-like eyes is seeing if she needs help. A hand appears next to the eyes, and it beckons her and motions to the front door of the house. They are offering her sanctuary, Wendy realises, and a warm feeling rises inside her at the stranger's offer, in the face of mortal danger. To offer to open your front door to a stranger in these circumstances, with the undead just across the road, are braveness and kindness personified.

Wendy, even with the tyre iron in her hand, clasps her two hands together in front of her and mouths the words "thank you," to the stranger, but then shakes her head to refuse the offer. She takes a mental note of the house number and promises herself that when this is all over, she will return to thank the stranger properly for their risky offer.

The eyes disappear from the window quickly once Wendy has refused their help, and she is forced to return to the problem at hand. How is she going to get around the open corner to the next road without drawing the undead horde's attention? Then something else grabs her attention. What she needs is a diversion, and on the good Samaritan's doorstep is something that might help her create one.

Two small stone bunny rabbits sit guarding the house's doorway. Could she throw them across the road to make enough noise and create her diversion? If she could hit a car and set off its alarm, she could, she decides.

Wendy quickly places the tyre iron gently on the ground and gets onto her hands and knees to crawl over to the doorstep to steal the two bunnies. She makes another mental note, while she is at it, to apologise to the owner when she returns in the future.

Back against the cover of the car, Wendy weighs up the stone figures in her hands for a moment to calculate how hard she will need to throw them. Satisfied she has a good idea, she moves to the front of the car and slowly rises to peer over the top of the bonnet to choose a target.

Her attention is stolen away from choosing a target for a moment, however, caught up in the horror of the undead across the road, and only meters away to her right. The hideous creatures on their feet have heads that dart from side to side, snarling as they go, looking for prey, their flowing movements exaggerated and chilling. There are other creatures, perhaps even more chilling, down on their hands and knees, crouched over bodies on the ground, the beasts feeding on the people catastrophically caught in their lair.

Wendy's heart goes out to the damned that the creatures feed upon, fear growing inside her. She realises that they are looking for any opportunity to hunt, and she is about to offer them one.

Forcing herself to put the carnage and threat out of her mind, she looks for a suitable target. *Perfect*, she thinks. Just across the road from her, and near the undead, is a very smart-looking Audi, almost new, she would guess. She would also guess it will have a super-duper alarm to go with its flash looks and what's more, the owner can clearly afford the repairs.

Taking aim from behind the cover of the car next to her, Wendy launches one of the stone bunnies into the air. She watches its trajectory as it arches through the air, her hand reaching to pick up the tyre iron ready for her dash around the corner when the alarm sounds. Wendy's shot is excellent and the bunny crashes onto the roof of the Audi with a loud, vibrating bang, the closest creature's heads flashing around at the source of the sudden noise. The creature's attention is quickly lost though, as the bang dissipates and the high-tech car alarm fails to sound.

"For fuck's sake," Wendy says to herself, swapping her last missile into her throwing hand, *so much for the super-duper alarm.* She aims again, this time for the side of the car, hoping its sensors will be more attuned there and she launches the last bunny. The tyre iron is in her hand when the stone figure smashes through the side window of the Audi, sending the car into a panic of high-pitched beeping and flashing orange light.

Bingo! Wendy thinks, and presuming her diversion will do its job, she makes her dash out into the open and around the corner.

Her legs move as quickly as she can muster as she traverses around the corner. She stays low and as close to the houses as she can, in the shadows, where the streetlights are at their weakest. As she reaches the crest of the corner, she risks a glance across the road to see if her movement has been spotted by the undead, and she is pleased to see the Audi's alarm is the only thing the creatures are interested in. Her confidence growing, Wendy straightens her back and powers around the corner and onto the adjoining road, knowing her destination is now within reach.

Wendy doesn't see the creature move from the shadows in front of her and into the glow of the streetlights until it is too late, and she runs into the same glow, unable to stop herself. Her terror slams on her brakes but her momentum is too great to stop her from careering straight into the beast. Wendy's arms whip up in front of her body in reflex, to protect herself from the heavy collision. She comes to a halt directly under the light of the streetlamp and knocks the startled creature backwards.

Unfortunately, the creature manages to catch itself from falling as it staggers backwards, and in a flash, gets its balance back and quickly regains its wits. Wendy's fear is paralysing as the creature steps forward, back into the light, so that it is face to face with her. The fearsome male beast's dead eyes fixed upon its prey, its arms rising threateningly and ready to attack Wendy, whose rage has left her, she feels only terror. The creature's mouth prises open and the beginnings of a chilling screech form in its throat—whether to terrorise Wendy even further or to call to its kin, Wendy doesn't know.

The ache of the tyre iron in her hand runs up her arm and into her brain, sparking her out of her paralysis. Her ears ring as the high-pitched screech hits them and she knows instantly that she must extinguish the noise before it attracts more of the undead. Her aching arm moves across her body in the same instant that the beast moves in for the kill. Wendy's arm whips upwards, her shoulder straining to bring the heavy metal tool with it, just as the beast closes in on her.

The tyre iron flies through the air and crashes into the side of the beast's head with a sickening crunch as it moves into range. Immediately, the Godawful high-pitch sound coming out of the beast's mouth is cut off as it is knocked sideways by the tyre iron smashing into its skull. The creature staggers to the side from the force of the blow, and Wendy leaps forward to run past the floundering creature, taking her chance to run. And run she does. Wendy sprints straight down the road trying to get away before the creature can regain its bearings.

A horrific screech echoes after her and she forces herself to run faster, knowing the beast has begun its pursuit. Without looking back, Wendy instinctively knows that other creatures have joined the hunt as more chilling noises reach her.

Her speed carries Wendy quickly to the next junction she needs in the road. A single-lane street branches off left on the opposite side, and she dashes through parked cars to reach it. She can't help but look back up the road as she runs across to see what she is up against, but straight away she wishes she hadn't. A pack of undead zombies is tearing in her direction, moving at an impossible rate of knots.

With burning legs, Wendy disappears into the street that connects with the one on which Bradley's house is located on, and for a moment, at least she is alone. Bradley's house is close, and she can see his road straight ahead of her, its bright streetlights shining in the darkness.

Not wanting to get close to the shadows and blind spots of the houses that line both sides of the street, Wendy sprints down the centre of the tarmacked road and in between the lines of parked cars. She nears the end of the road in no time, but not before she hears her hunting pack come around the corner to follow her.

Suddenly, she has brain freeze and can't remember if Bradley's house is on the left or the right at the junction that she is about to reach, and she can't afford to go in the wrong direction. *Right, it's on the right*, she tells herself as a dark figure strays into the middle of the road right in front of her. Her terror spikes at the sudden appearance, but she cannot slow down, as the pack is closing in behind her and one zombie is better than a pack of them.

The young man, who has clearly been drinking and is not a zombie, stumbles up the kerbside, going in the same direction as Wendy. How he has made it this far is anyone's guess, but his luck is about to run out if he doesn't get off the street, and now.

"They're coming… Run!" Wendy screams at the drunk as she passes him, not slowing to turn right and onto Bradley's road. The young man seems oblivious to any danger and waves at Wendy, slurring something to her as he sways on the corner of the junction. There is nothing Wendy can do for the young Christmas reveller, but that doesn't stop her feeling of guilt and horror as she leaves him behind to his fate.

All she can do is dive to take cover and hide behind Bradley's old estate car as she finally reaches his house. Her breathing is nearly as out of control as her spiralling emotions.

Chapter 19

Wendy's loud and heavy breathing doesn't disguise or save her from the young revellers' screams of terror, or the sound of his hideous death when the undead pack runs into him, hovering on the corner. She is forced to listen as the pack slaughters him and fights over his flesh that isn't enough to satisfy their insatiable hunger; the horrific sounds will haunt her forever.

Eventually, Wendy's breathing slows, in unison with the disgusting sounds of death dissipating as the pack feeds. Wendy is well aware that the undead will quickly exhaust the meat they have stumbled upon and the hunt will begin again. She cannot remain cowering behind Bradley's car.

Her head turns towards Bradley's house in trepidation—the house that looms over her, haunting her. This is the one place on earth she never wanted to return to, right beside her, its front door wide open to welcome her back.

The house beyond the open door is dark, and it fills her with fear to even contemplate going back inside, but she must. Matt is inside, down in the basement, trapped in her cage and expecting her help, with their nemesis Bradley waiting for his family's reunion.

It is time to give Bradley what he wants, Wendy tells herself as she begins to edge herself toward the house, keeping low behind the car and out of view of the feeding undead. Her heart is pounding through her chest as she climbs through the open door and into Bradley's evil lair.

The darkness envelops Wendy as she is forced to ease the front door closed, to shut out the outside world and the undead. She cannot afford the risk of any of the creatures wandering in through the open door, and cannot risk turning on a light that would attract their attention. She rests her back against the door as it gently closes, and gives herself a minute to calm her nerves and become accustomed to her new surroundings.

A deathly silence hangs in the house, and the quietness does nothing to help ease her dread at returning. Her two hands grip the tyre iron and bring it up tight to her chest to cuddle into, as if to reassure herself that she has the weapon. The heavy tool is one advantage, together with surprise, but even those two things might not be enough to defeat Bradley and rescue Matt.

Her eyes become accustomed to the darkness and they pick out a sliver of light crossing the hallway in front of the basement door. *At least the basement lights are on*, she tells herself as she takes her first step towards it. She steps very carefully and slowly, not wanting to give away her presence and the advantage of surprise. The basement door is ajar, she sees as she rounds the bottom of the staircase, its silhouette outlined for her by the dim light that penetrates in from the street.

Wendy's eyes fix onto the yellow light streaming through the gap in the basement door. Nothing breaks its beam, and so she is confident nothing is at the top of the stairs as her hand reaches to pull the door open. It opens silently, and Wendy sticks her head around the doorframe to peer down the stairs which she sees are empty. She stays where she is for a moment, listening for any sounds that could give her a clue about the situation in the room below. She hears nothing over the sound of her own breath that she is trying desperately to control.

With the tyre iron still clutched to her chest, Wendy moves around the doorframe and slowly begins to descend the stairs, trying not to make a sound, her feet gradually transferring her weight to each new step. Her heartbeat thunders in her chest as she reaches the bottom of the stairs. It pumps the blood loudly into her ears and head, convincing her that the sound will carry into the room beyond the stairs and give her away.

Wendy continues nevertheless, her right hand taking control of the tyre iron that she holds out in front of her as she rounds the corner and moves out into the basement.

Wendy's legs go weak, her left hand having to rise to help hold the tyre iron steady when she sees Bradley standing with his back to her, looming in front of the cage door. His saggy dead skin hangs from his bones and around his flabby buttocks, his testicles in shadow hanging low between his slightly parted legs. Wendy's hands tremble against the metal of the tyre iron as she takes in the scene, and then her eyes move to find Matt. She sees him behind the mesh of the cage, seated on her bed with his back against the wall, his head flopped forward as if he is asleep.

Wendy's presence must have stirred Matt though, because as she looks at him, his head starts to rise as if he has felt her come into the room. His eyes blink at Wendy as though he might be seeing an apparition, his confusion obvious. But that confusion quickly turns to reality and his head straightens instantly and turns to Wendy, his face full of joy at seeing her, but he is also shocked that she is there, and there alone.

Suddenly, frightened that Matt will make her presence known to Bradley, Wendy's left hand leaves the tyre iron so that she can put her finger over her lips to tell him to be quiet. And Matt *is* quiet. He doesn't make a sound but something has alerted Bradley to Wendy's presence, because suddenly, his body straightens and he starts to turn around. Wendy's panicked mind can only guess that Matt's head suddenly moving to look at her has killed her element of surprise, or has the monster felt her presence?

Whatever the reason, it is of little consequence now, and Bradley's hideous body inches around to face Wendy, her terror absolute. Bradley's contorted, disfigured face stares directly at Wendy as he straightens himself up so that he is standing, facing directly towards her. Once in position, his head tilts forward slightly, his eyes staying fixed upon Wendy. She is sure a knowing, grimaced smile spreads across his face in the instant before his lips open to bare his teeth at her, or is he performing a sick grin for her?

"Are you okay, Matt?" Wendy asks as her left hand returns to the tyre iron, and she brings it to the side ready to strike out at Bradley.

"Wendy what are you doing? Where are the police? Get out of here before he attacks you!" Matt begs.

"The police aren't coming; the infection has spread."

"Then leave me here. Go, Wendy, please."

"No, Matt, this has to end here and now." The confidence in Wendy's voice is belying her terror.

"Dad," Matt shouts, trying to regain the beast's attention as he jumps up on the bed to get to the wired mesh. "Dad, don't you hurt her," Matt pleads, and he bangs on the wire, anything to divert the beast's attention.

Matt's words and commotion are ignored by Bradley who snarls at Wendy, his mouth beginning to open. And then he rushes forward without warning, directly at Wendy, Matt screaming in the background. Wendy doesn't move. She stands her ground as the grotesque beast rushes at her, its arms stretching out to grab hold of her.

Wendy bides her time, just as she did only a short time ago with the creature under the streetlight. She waits until Bradley's ugly fucking head is within range before she swings the tyre iron. Wendy puts all of her strength into the swing that is aimed directly at his head as the beast comes at her. She envisages the thick metal smashing into Bradley's skull and knocking him sideways, but at the last second, Bradley's arm comes up to deflect her blow.

The bone in Bradley's arm crunches as the tyre iron hits it, but it is a glancing blow and the tool flies out of Wendy's sweaty hand to smash into the nearby basement wall before clattering to the floor.

The beast hits Wendy backwards with an almighty force, slamming her against the back wall of the basement, forcing the wind out of her. Bradley pins her against the wall, his snarling mouth spewing putrid air straight into her face as she tries to get her breath back. Wendy is defenceless, as the beast's strength is too strong for her to fight, and she can't move.

Bradley's face pushes against Wendy's, the beast's dried out skin like sandpaper against her cheek. *Why doesn't he bite me?* Wendy thinks, her anger finally rising as the beast toys with her. Something moves against the side of her face, and Wendy realises that Bradley is indeed toying with her, his tongue slithering across her face. "Fuck you, Jonathan Bradley," Wendy says, her anger turning to rage as the beast's face leaves hers, its mouth finally opening to sink its teeth into her.

Bradley's head comes down to strike, but Wendy's rage has returned with a vengeance and her fist shoots up from below and smashes into the beast's bottom jaw before his teeth can strike. Bradley's head whips back with a whimper but his fists close around Wendy's arms, and he picks her up clean off her feet and spins her through the air, throwing her against the adjacent wall.

Wendy's back again smashes against the wall and she falls to the floor in a pile, struggling to breathe once more. Before she can regain any semblance of composure, Bradley jumps on top of her and now pins her against the floor, his mouth primed to bite into Wendy's neck. Wendy's fight is lost, she realises, as the beast's head comes in for its strike, her rage useless against its power.

Matt races to untie the hammer, locking him into the cage as he sees his father knock Wendy back and pin her against the basement wall. Finally, the pressure is released from the hammer and he pulls it free from its jammed position through the mesh. The cage's door flies open as Wendy is thrown through the air, hitting the wall hard. Matt sees his father move in for the kill as he rushes out of the cage, the hammer raised in his hand.

Matt doesn't hesitate to bring the hammer down and smash it into the side of his dad's head, just as he is about to bite into Wendy. The beast is knocked sideways and off Wendy, whose eyes are wide and petrified as the beast topples off her. Matt leans down to his stepmother, grabbing her arms to pull her off the floor.

"Quick, Wendy, let's get out of here," Matt tells Wendy as her senses start to return from the abyss.

Wendy gets to her knees quickly, her head spinning; she thought her time had ended. She sees Bradley next to her on the floor, but her hope that he is dead is immediately extinguished as the beast writhes around, trying to get back up. Her eyes fall on the tyre iron next to Bradley where it fell from her grasp, and her hand reaches for it.

"Wendy, let's go!" Matt insists.

"Not yet," she tells him, picking up the heavy tool.

"Wendy?" Matt exclaims as she raises the tyre iron above her head and then brings it down with as much force as she can possibly muster. The metal crashes into the back of

Bradley's head, caving it in with a sickening sound of breaking bone. Instantly, Bradley's body goes limp as finally his life, and his undead afterlife, are killed once and for all.

Termination

Silence falls over the basement as Wendy releases the tyre iron, leaving it embedded in the back of Bradley's head. She doesn't move for the longest time as she lets it sink in that her monstrous husband is finally dead and cannot torment her any longer. Matt stands silently in disbelief over Wendy, his emotions in turmoil as he stares at his dead father.

"I'm sorry, Matt, but it had to be done," Wendy finally says.

"I know it did, there is no need to apologise," he replies.

"Good, then help me up please."

Matt helps Wendy to her feet, her battered and bruised body struggling, glad that this episode is finally over.

"What shall we do now?" Matt asks.

"I don't know, but we can't leave this house. There are zombies all over the city. Another thing we have to thank Bradley for," Wendy says, but immediately realises how insensitive her comment is, as Bradley was still Matt's father after all. "I'm sorry Matt, I didn't mean to sound insensitive, it's just been an ordeal."

"I know, Wendy, and I'm sorry for what he did."

"There is nothing for you to be sorry for, my love; this wasn't you. It was all your father, and you're not your father. It'll take time for us all to get over this," Wendy says, turning to Matt.

“Yes it certainly will,” Matt agrees.

“I think we are going to have to go upstairs and wait it out, until the authorities can regain control,” Wendy suggests.

“Yes, I think you’re right.”

Matt helps Wendy over to the stairs and they climb them wearily to go into the main house to recover.

“We will have to leave the lights off, I’m afraid. Creatures are in the streets and we don’t want to attract their attention,” Wendy tells Matt as they reach the hallway.

Just as Matt goes to close the basement door, a strange but familiar noise reverberates from behind it, the sound coming from the lounge.

“What was that?” Matt asks nervously.

“Where did Armstrong and his partner go?” Wendy asks quietly.

“I don’t know,” Matt replies.

“Quick, we’ve got to leave,” Wendy says urgently, pushing Matt toward the front door as a low whining noise comes to the open basement door from the lounge beyond. She knows the undead are in the streets, but what other choice is there but to leave the house? It has one of the undead inside it.

Matt opens the front door as the basement door behind them slams shut, and Wendy turns to see Armstrong’s partner Fleck in the shadows, racing towards them.

“Run,” Wendy cries out as Matt exits the house.

Wendy follows Matt out and onto the driveway, but the undead creatures she left on the street are still there. They instantly see them leaving the house, and move to intercept Matt and Wendy at the end of the drive. Behind them, Fleck reaches the doorway, where she stops to screech at the top of her voice when she sees her undead kin.

Trapped, Wendy and Matt look at each other in desperation with nowhere to go, knowing that even after all they have been through, they have no escape from the undead.

Suddenly, bright lights race up the street, followed by the sound of a revving engine. A camouflaged military vehicle appears and crashes into the undead on the streets, sending them flying into the air and tumbling across the road. Before either Wendy or Matt has time to react, the vehicle's doors slide open and military personnel pile out of the back. Gunshots ring out in all directions before Wendy even registers that the personnel are carrying weapons.

Fleck, still in the doorway, is shot to ribbons in seconds. And within the space of a minute, all the creatures in the area have been eliminated and a perimeter of soldiers surrounds the driveway, enclosing Wendy and Matt.

"Mrs Bradley?" one of the soldiers asks.

"Yes," Wendy replies.

"Where is Mr Jonathan Bradley?"

"He is in the basement inside. He's dead."

"Lieutenant, secure that body," the soldier orders one of his team. "In the vehicle please, Mrs Bradley, I have orders to take you to the FOB."

"FOB?" Wendy questions.

"Forward Operating Base, Mrs Bradley. Please, inside the vehicle. You too, son," the soldier orders Matt also.

"Why?" Wendy asks vacantly.

"We have intelligence that is ground zero for the outbreak, and we need to get you to a safe location."

Wendy suddenly thinks about the policewoman she gave her statement to at the police station. Maybe it wasn't a waste of time after all? Wendy and Matt get into the vehicle; there is no other choice, as the streets are too dangerous to stay where they are in any case.

As soon as they are inside, the door is slid shut and the driver turns the vehicle around before speeding off. On the way out of the city, they see military vehicle after military vehicle heading into the centre of Lemsfield. Wendy finds it hard to understand how the authorities have reacted so quickly.

She doesn't linger on it, however, as she is too exhausted to worry about it now. She leans against Matt next to her, to rest her tired and aching body. His arm moves around Wendy's shoulder and she closes her eyes, just for a minute.

If you have enjoyed ***CRUEL FIX,*** be sure to leave a review. Amazon reviews only take a minute and are so important in building a buzz for every book.

Many thanks, every review is appreciated!

For more information on Lance Winkless
and future writing see his website.

www.LanceWinkless.com

By Lance Winkless

THE CAPITAL FALLING TRILOGY

CAPITAL FALLING
CAPITAL FALLING 2 – DENIAL
CAPITAL FALLING 3 – RESURGENCE

THE Z SEASON – TRILOGY

KILL TONE
VOODOO SUN
CRUEL FIX

Visit Amazon Author Pages

Amazon US - Amazon.com/author/lancewinkless
Amazon UK - Amazon.co.uk/-/e/B07QJV2LR3

Why Not Follow

Facebook www.facebook.com/LanceWinklessAuthor
Twitter @LanceWinkless
Instagram @LanceWinkless
Pinterest www.pinterest.com/lancewinkless
BookBub www.bookbub.com/authors/lance-winkless

ALL REVIEWS POSTED ARE VERY MUCH APPRECIATED, THEY ARE SO IMPORTANT, THANKS

CAPITAL FALLING - THE TRILOGY: Books 1-3

***A #1 Bestseller – 800+ Pages* – Infectious to its Very Core**

As black smoke rises, order disintegrates . . .

Former SAS soldier Andy Richards is no stranger to horrors, but no training could ever have prepared him for the nightmare unfolding at home. While a viral epidemic hammers London, Andy finds himself trapped in the epicentre, forced to protect his family. Together with his young daughter, he leads a small group of survivors toward latent refuge, all the while searching for his missing son and infantryman; this is the ultimate game of survival.

With those infected displaying brutal, inhuman behaviour and caught up in a climate of martial law, no one can be trusted. Old connections may help to unravel this mystery virus, but the resultant hellscape means Andy and his group meet danger at every turn.

Stakes are high, and failing means a fate worse than death...

The perfect tale for troubled times, ***CAPITAL FALLING*** delivers dark thrills and surprising sentiment—twisted, cerebral fun. You'll race to the end like *your* life depends on it...

CAPITAL FALLING - CAPITAL FALLING 2 – DENIAL - CAPITAL FALLING 3 – RESURGENCE

★★★★★ A very well thought out storyline that leaves you wanting more... ★★★★★ Wow! A real Humdinger! ★★★★★ Loved the books, would recommend them to others. You need to give it a try!

Printed in Great Britain
by Amazon